KEEP ME GHOSTED

Keep Me Ghosted

Karen Cantwell

"Now, about those ghosts. I'm sure they're here and I'm not half so alarmed at meeting up with any of them as I am at having to meet the live nuts I have to see every day."
– Bess Truman

CHAPTER ONE

Marmaduke Dodsworth was good at many things, but probably his greatest talent was for talking my ear off. If I didn't clamp him down, he'd make me late for another interview.

After slipping my battered Honda into a space barely big enough for a Matchbox car, and punching the gear shift into park, I turned in my seat and ordered Marmaduke succinctly: "Stay here. Shut up." I pointed a stern finger in his direction for emphasis.

Marmi was offended. "Madame Sophie," he said, the words rolling elegantly from his British tongue, oozing slowly like sap from a maple. "I am not some mongrel to which you must command a 'stay.' Shall I roll over as well? Or would you like me to beg? More importantly, your second directive is rendered entirely moot, should I choose to obey the first, for if I were to 'stay here,' then surely, my 'shutting-up' would hardly matter. Why, I could continue to bang on about any number of subjects and you would be none the wiser."

Based on the context, I assumed "bang on about" meant pretty much the same thing as having diarrhea of the mouth, but I wasn't about to encourage further banging by asking for clarification. I'd have Marmaduke translate that British-ism another time. I did feel guilty for the harsh command, though.

1

He was right – he wasn't a dog in need of training. He was a couth, well-manicured, attractive, and upstanding man who, if circumstances were different, would have had relationship potential. Even though he wasn't exactly my type, romantically speaking, his dark hair, brown bedroom eyes, and firm jaw line had probably caused more than a few girls to swoon. What I loved about Marmi was his dry wit and, of course, that fun English accent. We had met during a particularly troubling time in my life and he'd proven to be a stalwart friend. Unfortunately, he had also proven to be so intrusive during my job quest that boundaries had to be set, or I was destined for certain destitution.

I checked my makeup in the rearview mirror, made a mental note that my new short hairstyle was in need of a trim already, then reached into the backseat for the résumé folder. "You're right. Talk all you want, but please, please, *please* stay here."

He huffed like a chastised child while straightening the lapels of his very dated suit jacket. "As you wish."

I studied his smooth, clear face for signs of defiance. "I'm serious. If I could lock you in, I would. You cost me that last interview."

"The man was a letch, a cad with no morals. No integrity. *Pond scum,* I believe is a term you have used to describe such filth. You can do better."

"I need a job, not a babysitter."

Marmaduke was obviously more hurt than offended by my last remark and that made me feel worse. I tried to make nice. "Dude, I'm sorry. Just stay here. Promise?"

He turned his gaze out the window, giving me the cold shoulder. "'Dude.' She calls me 'Dude.' What am I? A rootin' tootin' cowboy on the range?"

I rolled my eyes and closed the door behind me, worried that he neglected to promise anything.

As I crossed the parking lot, my heels clicking on the black macadam, I double-checked the address scribbled on the résumé folder. 2424 Granite Hills Drive, Suite A. Scanning the front of the two-story brick building in front of me, I saw Suites B, C, and D, but no A. My head bobbed back and forth from the folder to the building. Perplexed, my next plan of action was to pop into Suite B and ask for directions to the mysterious Suite A.

A voice in my ear caused me to flinch. "You look lost." It seemed that while I had been wishing for a GPS, a man had stepped up beside me from behind.

Still rattled by the suite confusion and worried about the interview, I gave him the briefest of glances. "Sort of." I pointed to the address on my folder. "I'm looking for Suite A. I don't see it."

"Sure. Know it well." He motioned with an elbow. "Follow me."

Doing as instructed, I shadowed the tall, lanky man who I now noticed was carrying a McDonald's bag in one hand and a cup of soda in the other. His tan dress pants and long-sleeved, white dress shirt told me that he probably worked somewhere in the business park himself. He ambled to the left side of the building and then around the corner, which was nicely shaded by a cluster of dogwood trees. The shade was a welcome relief since my car's air conditioning had gone belly up two weeks before the heat of summer arrived. I winced against the pain in my feet that were squished into a pair of heels that, in retrospect, were probably too high for an interview. But they went well with the business-like blouse and skirt ensemble. *Should have gone with the one-inch heels or the flats*, I thought.

Shifting the bag to his soda hand, he retrieved a set of keys from his pants pocket and proceeded to a glass-paned door. Above the door in black letters were the words *Dr. H.U. Callahan*, Optometrist. I sighed happily, thankful that the name, Dr. Callahan, matched the name on my folder. The tall McDonald's-eating guy had helped me find the right place. Now hopefully I wasn't late. I corrected my posture, checked the buttons on my blue interview-appropriate blouse, straightened the wrinkles in my black just-above-the-knee skirt, and did a quick finger-brush through my hair.

The man pulled open the door in front of us, and smiled. "After you."

I realized, in my haste and distraction, that I'd never really acknowledged him. I returned the smile and took in his face. It was a nice face. Pleasant. Friendly. He looked young – possibly an intern. Accepting his offer to go first, I stepped into the deliciously cool office. "Thank you," I said. "Do you work here?"

He laughed and cocked his head in a self-conscious manner. "That's the idea anyway."

The waiting room was small and not very tidy. Actually, it was a mess. The reception desk directly in front of me lacked a vital component – a receptionist. But, of course, that made sense, since I was there to apply for that very position. Stacks of papers were piled here and there on the desk and on the cabinets behind it, as if awaiting some form of organization. The possible intern moved around behind the desk, set his McDonald's stash down, then gave me another unsure sort of smile. He opened his mouth as if he was going to speak, but then, seeming to reconsider, shut it again and said nothing. *Oh boy,* I thought, *now I'm going to have to deal with Dr. Callahan's awkward assistant.* I put my hand out to introduce myself. "Sophie

Rhodes. I have an interview for the receptionist position. I was told to ask for Dr. Callahan."

He shook my hand so hard my elbow nearly dislocated. "Yes. Yes."

"Is he here?" My hand was beginning to ache.

"Yes." He turned his head to the side. "Not now," he mumbled.

The man kept pumping while my bewilderment grew. "Not now? I'm pretty sure I'd arranged—"

"Not you," he interrupted.

I extracted my nearly purple hand from his and scanned the room for signs of other life that he might be addressing. We were, it seemed, alone. Although I knew, better than anyone, that things were not always what they seemed. The teeny tiniest hint of a familiar sensation made me wonder, *is it possible?* I shrugged off the thought and returned my attention to the oddball intern. Although, really, he was kind of a cute oddball. Inviting face, light olive complexion, crooked smile, sparkly blue eyes. And, upon closer inspection, maybe a little older than I originally thought. "Uh," I continued. "Do you think you could tell him that I'm here?"

A look of understanding crossed his face. "I get it now." His head bobbed. "You're confused." More head bobbing. "My fault, my fault." He pointed to his chest. "I'm Dr. Callahan. I know you're here."

Ah geez. There, I'd gone and done it again – blown another interview. I must have looked like a complete idiot. I know I felt like one. Intern. Ugh. True, the baby-faced doctor seemed a little flaky, and I'd had my travails working for flaky people before, but man, I needed the money. Needed it bad. The situation called for immediate repair. I wouldn't bring up his young appearance – he was probably sensitive. "I'm so sorry..." I dove in. "I...guess I expected a doctor would be..." Seemingly possessed by some rash moment of utter stupidity, I began babbling about lab coats. "Wearing a lab coat. You know, doctors and lab coats." Crap. I should have gone with the your-baby-face-threw-me-off excuse. Who was looking flaky now? "I mean, don't doctors...you know...wear lab coats?" *Crash and burn, Sophie. You just crashed and burned.*

He sipped from his soda straw and eyed me with a cocked brow. "No." Another sip. "When can you start?"

Stunned that my lab coat obsession and inability to string a coherent sentence together hadn't hurt my chances for employment, I jumped on it. "I'm available immediately."

His shoulders relaxed and he released a healthy sigh. "Great." He pointed to some items on the desk. "Here are the phones. There's the appointment book. You're a life saver." He picked up his meal and started down the hall that led to the back of the suite.

"Wait!" I called after him. "What are you paying? What are the hours? Don't you want to know if I'm a crook who will rob you blind?"

He stopped and turned around. "Are you?"

I shrugged. "No."

He took two steps back in my direction. "You didn't look like a crook. How much do you want?"

Whoa. How much did I want? I'd never heard that one before. "You don't do this a lot, do you?"

"I'm not following you."

"You don't seem very experienced in hiring people. You never ask them what kind of salary they want. You tell them what you're paying."

"I've hired *lots* of people. I just can't seem to keep them from quitting." He pulled a limp fried potato from the bag. "French fry?"

The intoxicating scent of McDonald's fries did make my empty tummy rumble. But I shook my head to decline while wondering about the contents of that cup he was sipping from. Perhaps it was something more potent than soda. Like... rum maybe? "What happened to your last receptionist?" I asked him.

"Sheila. She left for a cigarette break. Never came back." He swallowed, then frowned. "Shoot. Fries are cold already."

"Are you hard to work for?" I asked, not that I expected him to say yes.

His light brown brows furrowed. "I don't think so. I try to be very accommodating." His shoulders slumped. "Sheila even set her own hours. I only saw patients when she could come in." His head turned slightly and he lowered his voice. "Not now."

His behavior was becoming suspicious, to say the least.

I narrowed an eye at him. "You said it again."

"What did I say?"

"'Not now.' You said, 'Not now,' out of context, like you're talking to someone else. Do you have Tourette's?"

His attention had wandered to the contents of his bag. "I wish it were that simple. They gave me two apple pies, you want one?"

Ah geez. I took a deep breath. "When is your next patient?"

"That's a good question." Setting down the bag and soda again, he brushed his hands together and grabbed the appointment book he'd pointed to earlier. He flipped through the pages, then pointed. "Four o'clock."

I looked at my watch. It was 12:20. "You're not very busy, are you?"

He nodded. "It's a problem."

I blew out a sigh, not believing myself what I was about to do. I reached up, took Dr. Callahan by the shoulders (noticing he would have been just the right height for a slow dance

7

partner), and guided him down into the rolling chair next to the desk. I had his attention. Planting a firm fist on my hip, I made my pitch. "I need sixteen dollars an hour. I'm worth it. And don't worry, I don't smoke. I'd like an hour for lunch. What hours do you want to be open?"

"Ten until six?"

"Good. I'll be here at nine-thirty and close up the office at six-fifteen. Monday through Friday?"

He nodded while his face relaxed with relief. I smiled inwardly when I noticed he was even cuter sitting down. Quite handsome, actually. Boyish good looks. Generally, I was attracted to darker, more rugged men with an edge to them, but this Dr. Callahan...there was something about him.

That's when she materialized. *Aha,* I thought. *That's who he was talking to. He has a ghost.* She must have read my mind. Her long, dark hair was bone-straight, falling far past her waist; her nose thin and elegant. Her clothing – a long, casual dress – was a current-day style, but her skin color and features told me she was Asian. Indian, I guessed. Her eyes were black as pitch and she narrowed them at me like a cat on the hunt. She wasn't happy that I was on the scene. Not one bit. She leaned into Dr. Callahan and whispered in his ear.

"What's she saying?" I asked.

He brushed his hand in the air near his ear as if driving away a gnat and gave me a surprised stare. "Excuse me?"

"Your friend there. What's she saying?"

Rolling his chair forward slowly, he whispered. "You mean, you see her?"

I cleared my throat and mimicked his hushed speech. "I have one too."

As if on cue, Marmaduke's voice sounded in my ear. "Sophie, dearest," he said. "We have a bit of a problem."

"Not now, Marmi." Poor ghosts. They get that a lot: "Not now."

My new boss didn't catch on very fast. "Who are *you* talking to?"

"Show yourself, Marmaduke." My spirit friend materialized as ordered – bowler hat and all. Dr. Callahan's jaw dropped. Having a spirit of his own, the good doctor didn't appear frightened the way most people probably would. But by his reaction, I guessed that the apparition draping herself over his body like hot fudge on a sundae was his first experience with the otherworldly.

Time for introductions. "Marmaduke," I said, "meet Dr. Callahan. Dr. Callahan, Marmaduke Dodsworth."

Unfortunately, Marmaduke was very protective of me and didn't offer an acknowledgement, pleasant or otherwise, to poor Dr. Callahan who kept swatting at the dark, disgruntled lady who floated around his head.

"Who's the queen of dramatics?" Marmaduke asked, with more than a hint of annoyance.

I crossed my arms, sizing her up. "Not sure yet."

"I'd love to hang around, as you Americans say, and acquaint myself more," Marmaduke sniffed sarcastically, eyeing Dr. Callahan and his attachment as if they smelled like rotten eggs, "but there has been an occurrence for which something must be done."

"You brought a ghost back from England?" asked Dr. Callahan. He looked Marmi up and down. "When were you alive, anyway?"

At first, Marmaduke scowled. I didn't expect him to answer, but he surprised me. "I was born on November seventh, eighteen hundred and eighty-four and I passed from the physical plane on the sad date of June first, nineteen hundred and fifteen, here, in your fair township of Stephens City. Struck down in the prime of my life by an automobile."

Dr. Callahan's eyes widened. He seemed impressed.

"We met at a bar," I added. "Long story."

"Sophie," Marmaduke pressed. "The occurrence..."

"Marmi, I just accepted this job, and now, as you can see, I have to contend with a ghost that doesn't seem to like me very much. Can't it wait?"

Marmaduke spoke out of the corner of his mouth, as if that would really keep the others in the room from hearing him. "Yes, well, waiting would be a problem. See, the bloke prefers the razzers be notified sooner rather than later."

There was no context for that word. I had to ask. "What's a razzer?"

"The police, my dear."

Something about his tone made me nervous about asking the next question. "And who's the bloke you're referring to?" I winced, waiting for the answer.

"The dead man in Suite C."

CHAPTER TWO

Apparently, the dead man in Suite C was now a ghost. In his new spirited form, "the bloke" had conversed with Marmaduke. "He was in that perfectly dreadful state. It is quite a trauma for a new ghost, you know. The disorientation. The discombobulation." Marmaduke shook his head. "I remember my own transition well. Bloody awful. You know that something is off, you just aren't sure what. First you are here, then you are there. You think to yourself, 'Am I down with a bitterly nasty case of the influenza? Am I hallucinating?'"

"Marmi," I urged him. "The man in Suite C. Can you get back to him?"

"Yes. Well, he appeared out of nowhere in the parking lot while I sat in that infernal box you call an auto car. He wandered aimlessly for a few moments, and realizing he needed some direction, I approached him and said, 'I hate to be the one to tell you this ol' chap, but you are quite dead.' It sounds harsh when I repeat it now, but sometimes you just have to be brutally honest about these things. He didn't respond immediately, but I felt it my duty as a comrade to see this apparition to some conclusion, whether it was escape into the light or at least awareness of his new state of being, as you will. Eventually, the fellow was able to recognize this building and even indicate a strong pull to Suite C. It was at that point that he truly understood he was dead, could picture his body, and became extremely agitated over its condition and treatment. We ghosts do that, you know. Care deeply about the bodies we left behind. The old boy really did wish that someone would call the authorities and let them know as soon as humanly possible. So his body wouldn't rot away like an animal carcass on the side of the road. See, the only thing he feels sure about is that he was alone when he expired."

The story could have been told in less than twenty seconds, but this was my bombastic Marmaduke, after all. He took more time and used more words than necessary, throwing in a touch of dramatic flair for added effect.

I was antsy to get to the bottom line, since obviously I would have to explain something to the police when I called them. "Where is he now?"

"He faded off. He might have passed into the light for all I know."

Even though I have a ghostly companion, I'm not an expert in all things spirit-related. Not even close. I mostly know what Marmaduke tells me – he says that right after death, if a spirit remains connected to the earthly plane, reality is hazy at first because time doesn't exist in their new dimension. Basically, the newly dead guy from Suite C was in a woozy state, if he was still around. Kind of like the time in college when I played the Star Wars drinking game using tequila shots. You know the one: throw back a shot every time a character says "Luke." I'm pretty sure my hazy state the next morning was very close to what a spirit feels like when it disconnects from a body. Minus the cotton mouth. And if that's the case, I felt really bad for the poor guy.

Dr. Callahan gave Marmaduke a long, hard stare, then posed a logical question. "What if we call the police and it turns out there's no body? I mean, he could have died weeks ago, right?"

"Are you addressing me, sir?"

"Yes."

"How should I know? I am merely a messenger. An envoy. A harbinger."

"You sound more like a thesaurus."

If Marmaduke had been a peacock, his feathers would have ruffled something fierce. He didn't respond to the thesaurus remark, probably because he was thrown off guard, but I suspected he was working on a zinger of a retort.

"Do you know how he died?" I asked.

"When my person walked the physical plane, I was a banker, fair Sophie, not Sherlock Holmes."

I loved Marmi, but his inability to answer a question with a simple "yes" or "no" was irksome.

Meanwhile, I'd been so focused on Marmaduke that I hadn't noticed that Dr. Callahan's ghost had vanished. And he wasn't swatting at the air. I was about to ask him if she'd left or just gone invisible when she reappeared.

"Oh, yippee. It's Dawn of the Dead joining us again. I am so terribly honored, aren't you, Sophie?"

"Just checked Suite C," she sighed, not seeming to be bothered by Marmaduke's comment.

"And?" I asked.

She pretended to ignore me and spoke only to Dr. Callahan. "Dead guy alright."

"Her manners leave something to be desired," Marmi sniffed. "Does she have a name? Something by which we can address her other than 'Hey you'?"

"This is Moonflower. She came with the office. I think," Dr. Callahan said. "Should we be calling 911?"

"And tell them what?" I asked. "That two ghosts have confirmed a dead body is lying in Suite C?"

He shrugged. "I can just tell them that I heard something suspicious."

"That office isn't close enough for you to hear something suspicious unless someone took him down with a nine millimeter handgun at the very least. We should probably walk up there and accidentally find him."

Dr. Callahan lifted his soda cup. "You seem to know a lot about these things." He sucked on the straw until the tell-tale slurping sound indicated that he'd emptied his supply. He shook the ice around and slurped some more, just to be sure.

"If you had read my résumé, you would have seen that I worked for the Stephens City Police for two years. I have a little experience in this area, unfortunately."

No one wanted to do this less than I did. Chances were good that when the squad car arrived, I'd know the guy driving. I had wanted to leave my police life behind me with the heartache, but that just wasn't happening.

So up we marched to Suite C, Moonflower hanging on Dr. Callahan like a honeymooning bride, and Marmaduke chattering on about something. I wasn't really listening since I was more engrossed in sizing up the doctor. At first he had seemed odd enough that his more appealing features were lost on me. Now I was keenly aware of his confident stride, not to mention the feathery straw-colored hair that showed blond highlights when the sun hit it just right. And a hint of a dimple that puckered on his left cheek when he squinted against the sun. He smelled good too. I wasn't sure if it was cologne or the soap he used, but either way, I was definitely finding myself a tad attracted.

Marmaduke whispered in my ear, evidently aware that I was ogling. "Did you say you accepted the position working for this bloke?"

"Yes."

"Is it wise then, to mix business with pleasure?"

I'd grown accustomed to Marmi's jealous nature. Even though he was a ghost and I was not, it was obvious that he had a little crush on me. Consequently, he always had a reason why this man or that man was "not fitting." Unfortunately, he'd called this one right. I couldn't even consider an attraction, much less a relationship, with my boss. In my younger years, I would have been careless and said *What the heck?*, but having been around the block a few times at the age of twenty-nine, I was going to take the mature path and sweep any idea of romantic possibilities right out the door. Besides, who needed a romantic entanglement with a man whose ghost wanted me out of the picture? Marmaduke was right. I needed to nip this blossoming temptation in the bud before it grew into a weed too tough to pull.

We arrived in front of the door to Suite C, which appeared identical to that of Dr. Callahan's Suite A, except for any shade from dogwood trees. The letters on the brick above read, *Stephens City Realty, Ronald Ellison, Agent.*

Dr. Callahan pulled on the door, but it didn't budge.

"Can you see anything inside?" I asked. Not waiting for an answer, I stepped beside Dr. Callahan and peeked through the glass. I had to cup my hands and use them as shields against the bright sun that reflected back at me.

The office appeared wider than Dr. Callahan's, but neater. A waiting room was furnished with black leather armchairs and a ficus tree that stood in one corner. A hallway led back with just one door visible on the left wall. What I did not see, however, was a body – dead or alive.

"You wouldn't see him from there, Johnny." Moonflower sighed, then floated through the glass and to the closed door on the hallway wall. I envied that ghostly ability to travel through walls and barriers. Don't get me wrong – I like my body and love being alive, but really, how cool would it be to just walk through a wall?

Moonflower pointed to the door, which I guessed meant that the body of the dead man lay behind it.

"Now what?" Dr. Callahan asked.

Good question. With no evidence of an accident or crime and no reason to be suspicious, what would we say when we called 911? While I pondered our dilemma, a gold Mercedes rolled slowly around the upper corner of the parking lot and turned into a space right in front of us. The driver, a woman with thin, blunt-cut, shoulder-length hair and harsh bangs climbed out of the front seat, eyeing us warily. "Can I help you?"

Dr. Callahan cleared his throat and spoke in a cracking voice. "We were looking for Ronald Ellison, but the door is locked. Do you know if he's around?"

"The door's locked? Are you sure?" She slammed the car door and stomped, pushing through us. She yanked on the doorknob. When it didn't open, she fiddled through the ring of keys in her hand until she found one she liked, inserted it into the dead bolt and yanked again. When that didn't help her open the door, she blew out a frustrated breath, found another key, jammed it into the doorknob and turned again. "Why exactly were you looking for him?" she asked, pulling the door open successfully this time. "Did you have an appointment?"

I cringed inwardly, knowing this woman was about to make a grisly discovery. "No appointment," I said, winging it as we followed her into the waiting room. "Just making inquiries. You are?"

"Dory Ellison, his wife."

"Excuse me one moment," said Mrs. Ellison. She disappeared around the corner.

I held my breath, expecting the worst.

Dr. Callahan leaned toward me and whispered. "Do you think she'll scream?"

Trying to ignore the pleasant thoughts his tantalizing aroma elicited, I shrugged and peeked down the hallway to see Dory Ellison returning with a smile on her face. She'd come from a different office down the hall – not the infamous death-room.

"I don't know why he isn't here," she said, her face crinkled in bewilderment or dismay. It was hard to tell which. "He must have walked to the McDonald's for lunch, although I will say, the timing couldn't be worse." She heaved an annoyed sigh, answering my question – dismay. She was definitely dismayed. But not for long apparently, because the crinkles disappeared like magic when she flashed a photo-ready smile. "How can I help you? Are you wanting to buy, sell, or rent?" Evidently, Dory Ellison didn't let a little thing like a missing husband get in the way of a potential business deal.

Dr. Callahan's eyes flicked to Moonflower. "Do something," he said through clenched teeth.

Moonflower smiled. "Anything for you, Johnny." She floated off, through the wall again.

Mrs. Ellison was confused. "I'm not sure I understand. Mr..."

"Doctor," he said, "Doctor Callahan. I wanted to do something... new."

Maybe the man wasn't good at fibbing on the spot. "Dr. Callahan is the optometrist around the corner in Suite A," I said, stepping in. "He was just wondering what kind of rent he could get for his office space."

"I know that office. But didn't you just move into that space a couple of months ago?"

Oops.

A loud crashing sound reverberated from the mysterious room. So, I thought, Moonflower can move mass. According to Marmaduke, not all ghosts were capable of such a feat. I was impressed. She still annoyed me, but I was impressed all the same.

All heads turned to the closed door.

"That's strange..." Mrs. Ellison's voice trailed off as she took a few tentative steps in that direction. When she wrapped her hand around the doorknob, I cringed again, knowing the discovery was certain this time. Moonflower was floating through the wall, just as Mrs. Ellison entered the room. I didn't even count one-Mississippi before hearing the predictable, ear-splitting scream.

"Ronald! Oh! Oh, dear! Help!"

Dr. Callahan reacted immediately to Mrs. Ellison's call for help, and I was right on his heels. With the chivalry of a confident knight, he knelt beside Ronald Ellison's body which lay face up on the brown carpet. He put a finger to the man's throat, then an ear to his chest. Mrs. Ellison knelt on his other side, shaking her poor dead husband. The forced motion bounced Dr. Callahan's head around while he listened for signs of life. She yelled at me to call 911, but I was way ahead of her, dialing my cell phone while she continued to shake Ronald. "Wake up, wake up!" she moaned.

While I gave information to the emergency dispatcher, I scanned the room, wondering if Ronald might appear at his wife's request. If he did, he wasn't allowing me to see him. When the dispatcher hung up, I whispered to Marmaduke. "Is he here now?"

Marmi shook his head. "No such luck, as you young Americans like to say."

"I'm sorry," Dr. Callahan said to the distraught woman on the floor. "He's... well... I mean... he's not alive."

She stopped suddenly, as if slapped. "He's dead?"

"That's... well... yes."

She looked at her husband, then back at Dr. Callahan. "You're a doctor, save him!"

Dr. Callahan blinked. "I'm an optometrist, not an ER doctor. Eyes." He pointed to his own frantically. "I do eyes."

Mrs. Ellison didn't seem to care. "Do you know CPR?"

It was obvious to me that as heroic as he'd like to be, Dr. Callahan knew Mr. Ellison was beyond hope. "Yes, but—"

"Then do it!" she shouted. "Save him! He can't die."

Dr. Callahan shot me a what-do-I-do-now look, but I was short on bright ideas. I shrugged.

"I don't know," he answered. "I mean, he feels kind of cold to the touch. I'm pretty sure he's...gone."

Like a spine-tingling scene in a horror flick, Mrs. Ellison's face morphed instantly from distraught to possessed-by-the-devil raging, and her voice lowered at least a hundred octaves. "Do it!" she growled.

Probably fearing for his own life at this point, Dr. Callahan got to work, tilting Ronald's head back, loosening his shirt, and checking his airway for obstructions. I felt badly for him. It's one thing to know you're saving a person's life when you go in for mouth-to-mouth, but it can't be pleasant to know you're going to be swapping saliva with a corpse. His face went from white to green as he bent down to give the first breaths.

"My, my," Marmaduke said with a smile. "Look who decided to join us in this rousing festival. Or should I say, a-rousing?" He nodded toward the corner of the room where Ronald the ghost stood, holding a perplexed expression on his transparent face. It was then, too, that I noticed Moonflower had disappeared.

During the first set of chest pumps, Ronald the ghost moved in closer to his body, eyeing it with interest. Then he looked up at Marmaduke. "What's your guess? You think I can bring that sucker back to life?"

Marmi chuckled. "I must say, I have never seen it done myself, although I've heard tales that it is possible."

"What sort of odds do you give me?"

Marmi shook his head dismissively. "I am not a betting man, sir."

I was stunned. Was this ghost really going to attempt to revive his own body?

"How about you, cutie?" The ghost of Ronald Ellison winked at me. "You think I can pull this off?"

Without thinking, I answered him out loud. "Do you really want to try? What if there's brain damage?"

Assuming that I was addressing him, Dr. Callahan stopped pumping Ronald's chest. "That's a very good point, Sophie. We should consider the possibility of brain damage."

"Don't stop!" roared the wife.

Obeying, Dr. Callahan pumped twice more, then moved into position, plugging Ronald's nose and poising to give another breath. Simultaneously, Ronald smiled a devious smile, laid over his own body and disappeared. It was right then, while Dr. Callahan and Ronald Ellison were lip-locked, that the dead man coughed and resurrected. It was also right then that Dr. Callahan screamed like a girl, and fell backwards on his rump, horror stricken. I have to admit, the scream sort of ruined the whole chivalrous knight thing for me briefly, but he recovered quickly, and really, who wouldn't scream when a dead man coughs in your mouth?

"Maybe I should have taken that wager," said Marmaduke, obviously impressed.

And as we all heard the first howl of sirens in the distance, Dory Ellison slapped her husband hard on the face. "You idiot!" she screamed. "You're missing the Williams closing!"

CHAPTER THREE

D ory Ellison's bizarre reaction might have been more awkward if the sirens, now blaring loudly, hadn't distracted us. I
took advantage of the interruption to run out the front door and
make sure they found the right office suite. Then I convinced
Dr. Callahan that we should get out of everyone's way and head
back to his office. He did have a patient at four o'clock, after all.
Even though it was only 1:15 by my watch, that left me quality
time to train up in my new job. Marmaduke said he would stick
around and watch the Ellisons to see how things unfolded.

"Did you see that?" Dr. Callahan beamed as we walked back
to his office. "I saved a man's life."

I didn't want to let him down and tell him that it wasn't
his expert CPR techniques that breathed life back into Ronald
Ellison's body. "You sure did," I agreed, smiling when his chest
puffed a little more from pride in the accomplishment.

Back at the office, we found Moonflower pouting in a
reception room chair.

"Why did you leave?" I asked her.

Ignoring me, she stood and raised her nose in the air.
"Johnny, can we speak privately?"

He rolled his eyes and I detected frustration. "Not that I
have a choice," he said, and strolled down the hallway with
Moonflower following.

She stopped for just a minute to turn back and shoot me an evil stare. "I don't like you," she hissed.

"We'll call it mutual then," I responded.

I hadn't had a tour of the place to know exactly where they were going, but I guessed it was one of his examining rooms. After locating an instruction manual tucked away in a drawer, I taught myself how to use the phone and messaging system. Unfortunately, one of the messages was from his four o'clock patient wanting to reschedule, which I managed to do successfully for the next day. I remembered that my own doctor and dentist gave me reminder calls the day before my own appointments, and figuring that this office could use all of the help it could get, decided to do the same. My first three calls went to voicemail, so I left messages letting them know we looked forward to seeing them the next day. My fourth call was answered by a nice lady named June who seemed surprised at the reminder. She remarked that I was, "much friendlier than that last receptionist. She was a monster."

The computer seemed to be logged into a billing program, so I went searching through drawers again for another user's manual. Five minutes of searching proved fruitless, so I decided to ask the man himself. As I made my way down the long hallway from the reception desk, I noted a tiny cubicle of a kitchenette on the left followed by a bathroom just two more steps down the hall.

The door to the first room on my right was open and the light was off. I flipped the light switch on the wall, illuminating a large room with two computers on tables, each up against a different wall, a large TV screen on another, an open cabinet filled with what looked like toys, and a rectangular table in the middle with a chair positioned on each side. A few plastic crates were scattered around on the floor that were overflowing with odd items I couldn't have identified if I wanted to. It seemed like a strange assortment of items for an optometrist's office. Where were the eyeglasses?

The next room on the right had a door that was closed. Not seeing another option, I knocked.

"Come in!"

I opened the door and peeked my head in, not wanting to appear too forward. "Dr. Callahan?"

I scanned the room, which, by the equipment, verified my guess: examining room. A large chair, well-worn as if it had seen years of experience, sat at the far end of the room. Attached to it, like an electronic octopus, were three or four metal arms holding instruments that looked more like what I would expect in a doctor's office. Pen in hand, Dr. Callahan sat on a rolling stool at a long gray desk full of drawers. The desktop, much like the reception desk, overflowed with papers and boxes and devices.

He smiled and shook his head. "Please don't call me that."

"What should I call you?"

"My friends call me Cal."

"Your name is Cal Callahan?" Then I remembered the initials on the signage above his door: H.U. "What do the initials stand for then?"

A frustrated expression crossed his face. "My legal name – don't laugh – is Hiram Ulysses Callahan. I'm named after our ancestor Ulysses S. Grant, whose real name was Hiram Ulysses. It's a long boring story, even to people related to him. Bottom line: my friends call me Cal."

Actually, I wasn't very comfortable calling him Cal. Dr. Callahan seemed much more professional, but I didn't want to offend him during our first day of working together.

"Of course," he said with a self-conscious head bob, "You should probably call me Dr. Callahan around patients."

I nodded, relieved. I couldn't help but joke though. "You mean I can't call you Johnny?"

His smile returned and he released a short chuckle. "What's that all about, right?"

"You don't know why she calls you Johnny?"

He rolled the pen between his fingers. "No idea." When he ran his fingers through his hair, I found myself wanting to do the same. It wasn't thick, but it wasn't too thin either. Nice hair. Sexy hair. Dr. Callahan's combination of clean-cut handsome and slightly awkward was very appealing to me for some reason. Maybe I was growing up. I reminded myself of Marmaduke's advice, and yanked myself back to the conversation.

"Interesting name she has there. Moonflower?" I asked.

More uncomfortable head bobbing. "She says she's not sure it was her name – you know – when she was..."

"Alive?"

He nodded. "I'm a doctor, you know. The sciences are what I know. Facts. Reality. This is all..."

"You've never had a ghost companion before?"

"Ha! Are you kidding me?" He gave me a quizzical look. "You sound very experienced. How many have you had?"

I leaned against the door jam. "When I was five, I had an 'imaginary friend.' Her name was Beatrice. It wasn't until Marmi came along a year ago that I realized she wasn't imaginary at all. So I'm not all that experienced. Sometimes it gets annoying. You know – he's always there. But on the other hand, we've become friends, so it can be nice to know that he's always there. So, what did you mean when you said Moonflower came with the office?"

His answer was interrupted by a ringing phone.

Excited to be doing an actual job for actual money, I jumped to attention. "Hold that thought," I said while running to the front phone.

We never had the chance to finish that conversation because after I handled the phone call, a mother and her son walked in, thinking they had an appointment. Dr. Callahan gladly took the son in while the mother read on her Kindle in the waiting room.

Marmaduke returned while I tried to figure out the patient filing system. "So the good doctor has patients after all? How nice for him," he said, spinning his bowler hat like a teenager with a basketball.

Since I couldn't respond verbally without looking like a crazy lady to the mother waiting, I opened a blank document on the computer and started typing. This was our default method of communicating when in public, although I usually typed on my cell phone as if I was texting. It always worked well except for the time on a subway train when a medium, aware of Marmi's presence, attempted to move him into the light. Marmaduke had avoided the light for a good 97 years; he wasn't about to let a rogue medium mess with his comfort zone.

I pointed to the screen and started clicking on the keyboard, anxious to learn if Marmi had more information about the Ellisons. Especially the dead/not-so-dead one. *What happened down there?* I typed.

"The Ellison fellow was carted away by ambulance."

Did he say anything? Remember anything?

"It didn't appear so. He was disoriented and fairly unaware of what had happened. He saw me though."

How do you know?

"He focused on me – it is very easy to recognize. If I had to guess, however, he did not remember being a spirited one himself. On this, I could be wrong, but it's unlikely. I'm rarely wrong."

Anything else?

"Anything else you ask? I'll say. Two razzers arrived on the scene and engaged in a conversation of some interest possibly to you and your new employer."

Police officers?

"They arrived soon after you departed with your new employer. Friends of yours."

Who?

"Alex."

That's only one. Who else?

"Shane. That dastardly Shane. Foul, foul excuse for a man. I felt like giving him a good scare."

Shane Daniels. I had a feeling. Ex-boyfriend and the reason I finally quit my job at the Stephens City Police Department.

How did he look?

"Truthfully, Sophie? How did he look? Like the ill-mannered gorilla he has always been. You are so much better than that beast. But you haven't asked me about their conversation of interest. Stay focused."

Don't get tongue-tied now, Marmi. Keep talking.

"Apparently, they were called to this same office building a little over a year ago. A young woman was found dead in a suite where her father operated an accounting business. She was Indian by lineage, and you guessed it – she was found in this very office. Probably right where you are sitting now."

Moonflower?

"Well, they only referred to her as 'that Indian girl,' but you and I have made similar assumptions. It really isn't a giant leap now, is it?"

The Kindle-reading mother interrupted. "You sure do stay busier than his last receptionist," she said.

I looked over the desk. "Just trying to catch up. He hired me on the spot today, and I'm sort of training myself."

"Dr. Callahan is a wonderful man and a great doctor. My son, Jason, loves him. I hope you actually stay around long enough to help him. The last lady talked on the phone all day with her friends and creditors. The one before that was more interested in her fingernails than making appointments and helping patients."

"Trust me, I need the job. I'll do my best to keep this one. It sounds like you come here often – is that normal, to see an eye doctor so regularly?"

"You really are training yourself, aren't you?"

"He's been... busy."

"Dr. Callahan is a developmental optometrist – he does vision therapy." She waited to see if the last words meant anything to me.

I shook my head. I'd never heard of vision therapy.

"Jason comes once a week – sometimes twice. Dr. Callahan trains him to use his eyes better." She rolled her eyes at herself. "That's not the right word..." She snapped her fingers a couple of times while thinking. "Efficiently!" She clapped her hands, happy. "That's the word I was looking for. Efficiently. He's learning to use his eyes more efficiently. He has trouble reading. Following words on the page. Tracking is the term Dr. Callahan uses."

"I did notice that most of his patients were children."

"It's a specialized form of optometry. My husband and I are so thankful – Jason went from being two grade levels behind in his reading skills to being a half-year ahead of grade level. And his grades in other subjects went from C's and D's to A's and B's. Honestly, it was like a miracle. And like I said, it helps that Jason loves Dr. Callahan the way he does. The man seems to have a way with kids. I've talked to some other mothers here in the waiting room. They agree."

"My, my, my," Marmaduke drawled. "A regular saint, this man is."

Marmi actually turned a ghostly shade of green.

"So," the nice mother continued, "I hope you'll stay and really help him whip this new office into shape. I'd send more patients his way if I wasn't so worried about how they'd be treated by his office staff."

Aha. The perfect time to learn about this history of Suite A. "When, exactly, did Dr. Callahan move into this office?"

She looked into the air, as if looking at an imaginary calendar. "Let's see. This is July. It must have been mid-April? He was sharing a tiny little office with two speech therapists about three miles from here, but their lease ran out I guess. He was very excited when he was able to buy this place. He said he got a great deal on it. Evidently, the previous owner suffered a terrible loss and wanted to be rid of it as quickly as possible."

I wondered if the 'terrible loss' was Moonflower. "Boy, he sure does share a lot of information with his patients."

"I work with his mother," she winked. "She likes to talk about her only son."

I made a mental note to talk more with Jason's mother if I wanted to know anything about Cal. I mean, Dr. Callahan.

A door swooshed open and the next thing I knew, Jason was tearing past the reception desk to his mother's side. Dr. Callahan moseyed out behind him with a patient file in his hand and a smile on his face.

"Let's go, Mom!" Jason bellowed, tugging at her arm. "I don't want to miss my show."

Looking at Dr. Callahan, I worked to get a grip on my duties. "Should I take a payment from her? Do we bill her insurance?"

He shook his head while handing me Jason's patient file. "She paid for his visits in advance. We're good. I'll show you the billing program and fee slip tomorrow." He waved to the departing mother and son. "Bye, Jason. Good luck with your soccer game tomorrow." He narrowed one eye at Jason, but held onto the smile. "Remember to practice those eye exercises I gave you today, right?"

Jason stopped. "And if I do, I can play the computer games?"

Dr. Callahan gave him a nod. "Just like I promised."

A large smile erupted across Jason's face and he ran out the door, his mother following.

"See you next week!" Dr. Callahan called with a final wave.

When the door closed behind them, he leaned an arm on the desk.

I pressed a palm to my forehead to push away a brewing headache. "Jason's mom sure did have some nice things to say about you." I looked at the folder he had handed me. "Should I file this away?"

"Yes please. Do you feel okay?"

"Just a little headache. I get them when I'm on the computer for a while."

"Hmm." He eyed me seriously. "And when you read – a book or a magazine?"

I had to think about that one for a minute. "Um, yeah. I guess so. Probably."

"I should give you an eye exam."

Poking through the filing cabinet behind the desk, I rifled through files until I located the proper spot, then slipped Jason's file in where it belonged. "I have twenty-twenty vision."

"Who's the doctor here?"

I laughed. "Jason certainly thinks you're cool as doctors go."

He fidgeted with a cup of pens on the desk. "Jason's a great patient. Good kid. He's done really well. And speaking of doing really well, you seem to be taking charge up here."

"That's why you hired me."

"It's not what I do best..." he waved his hands around my work area. "This stuff. I like seeing patients, working with the kids. Paperwork, phones – not so much. So I'm sorry for kind of, you know, dumping it all on you. And thank you for not taking a permanent smoking break. I *really* appreciate that."

"Well," I said, sitting back down. "We'll probably make a good team then, because I'm not so good with the kids, but I kick butt when it comes to paperwork and phones."

Dr. Callahan leaned further over the counter, moving the cup of pens out of his way. He cleared his throat. "There's one other thing..." breaking our eye contact, he cut his gaze down to the desk and cleared his throat again. "Something I wanted to ask you."

Suddenly, Moonflower appeared again, floating around him. "Johnny..." He stood upright and took a stern tone. "Not now, Moonflower. I need to ask Sophie something."

"But Johnny..."

He wasn't backing down. "Not now, I said. Not *now*."

"Sophie," Marmaduke whispered in my ear, "can I speak with you privately?"

"Marmi... Dr. Callahan needs to ask me something."

"That's what I'm afraid of," he whispered in response.

"That's enough!" Dr. Callahan shouted.

Marmaduke and Moonflower stopped their antics and I suppressed a smile.

"You two nosy ghosts," he pointed to the far corner of the room. "Over there."

When they didn't move immediately, he stressed his point. "Now."

Sheepishly and reluctantly, they moved away. "I'm impressed," I said, once they were far enough away to know that he'd achieved his goal.

"They're a pair, aren't they?" he snickered.

I laughed as I watched them in the corner sizing each other up with a good amount of indignation.

Dr. Callahan tried to lean on the counter again, but slipped a little. When he regained his composure and a better, more confident stance, he cleared his throat. "Let's try this again."

His tension led me to believe that he wasn't going to ask for my previous employer references. I held my breath. Was he going to ask me out? Part of me liked the idea. The other part of me said, *No, no, no, Sophie, bad idea! He's your boss! Your brand new boss!*

"I was wondering," he continued, "if you were doing anything tonight."

CHAPTER FOUR

And there it was. My boss of only five hours had just asked me on a date. If I hadn't found him attractive, I could have considered the move sexual harassment. I needed time to think, so stalled with an admittedly lame comment. "That's not really a question you know."

"What?"

"Technically, that would be a statement."

"Could you just pretend that it was a question?"

"See, now that's a question."

"Do you always make things this complicated?"

"To make another statement, I'm not sure that we should be dating. I just started working for you and..."

"Dating?"

"Aren't you asking me out on a date?"

"Good God, no. No!" He pulled back from the desk. "Is that what you thought?"

My face began to burn. "Now I feel really stupid."

He waved his hands at me. "You shouldn't feel stupid, I should feel stupid. Not that you aren't someone I'd enjoy – I mean, you're very... "

"What *did* you mean?"

He looked relieved that I stepped over his awkward moment. "Right. A meeting. I meant to say that there's a meeting I thought you'd find helpful. Tonight. It's a support group."

"Support group for what?"

"People like us." He motioned to Marmaduke and Moonflower. "You know, people with friends." He sighed. "Like ours."

They had a support group for people with ghost companions? Now that was a meeting I wanted to attend.

After showing me how to close out the financials for the day, giving me my own set of keys and instructing me on the alarm, we found ourselves outside making arrangements to meet at the Stephens City Community Center at seven o'clock. "There's a really nice sandwich shop next door – they make a fantastic chicken salad sandwich. Would you like to meet there first for some dinner?"

I hesitated. "I don't know..."

"Right," he nodded. "That would be too much like a date."

"Right."

"Understood." He nodded some more. "We wouldn't want to do that. I guess."

"No. No, we wouldn't."

"See you at seven then."

"Seven. For the support group."

"Not a date."

"Not a date."

Once I was finally in my car and buckled in, Marmaduke had to weigh in. "That was the most unusual and awkward mating dance I have ever witnessed in my life or my afterlife."

"Mating dance? What do you mean?"

"Do not play coy with me. You understand my meaning just fine. Not since the spontaneous eruption of infatuation between Romeo and Juliet have two people become so instantly enchanted with each other."

"Infatuation is a strong word, Marmi. You're being very melodramatic. Yes, maybe I find him a little cute—"

"Puppies and kittens are cute. Baby elephants are cute. You don't find him cute, you are smitten like Cleopatra was smitten with Mark Antony, like Penelope was smitten with Odysseus, like—"

"Would you stop? Besides, even if I find him attractive, the feeling obviously is not mutual."

"You can continue on this path of self-deception, but the very fact of the matter is that Miss Moroseflower is jealous for very good reason. There. I have said my piece. Now, what is this meeting and what is a community center?"

My wallet contained exactly nineteen dollars and thirty-two cents. That didn't count the Canadian nickel and two twenty-nine cent stamps. I had about ten dollars in the bank and maybe (if I was lucky) ten dollars available on my credit card. With this, I needed to eat and pay for gas. Taco Bell was always good for a cheap, unhealthy meal, so I made a pit stop at the drive-thru and ordered a burrito and a small Dr. Pepper. While I waited, I suffered in the heat and rehearsed asking Dr. Callahan when I would receive my first paycheck.

The Stephens City Community Center wasn't that far from my apartment, so I swung home first to make a quick change into more comfortable clothes and to feed and give some love to the other companions in my life.

Technically, Bayberry Arms Apartments only allowed one pet per apartment with a two-hundred dollar deposit, and then, tenants were limited to one dog under twenty pounds or one cat. I had pets, but I had never paid a deposit. That's because I also had a friend in the on-site manager, Mr. Franklin, who lived across the hall. As long as my pets kept quiet, so did he.

My cat, Uno, was a rescue from the Stephens City Animal Shelter. He only had one eye, but what he lacked in peripheral vision, he made up for in heart. I often found him waiting for me at the door when I'd arrive home. And anytime I sat on the couch, he'd hop up and curl in my lap more like a small dog than an independent and finicky feline. I think he knew that I plucked him from the edge of certain demise, since the one reason I chose him over the others was the fact that he was scheduled for extermination the next day.

The other animal in my life lived in a cage and spent a lot of time running out his energy on an exercise wheel. Mr. Franklin thought he was a genetically mutated hamster the first time he saw the creature with the bulging eyes and furry tail. I could understand his confusion. When I first found Peter Pan, I didn't know what he was either. It took some intensive internet searching to determine he was a baby flying squirrel. The best I could figure, he had fallen from his nest in my grandfather's yard. I had visited my Grampy and found him on the ground under a tall oak tree. Thinking he was a dead mouse, I scooped him up onto a piece of cardboard intending to dispose of him. But when the little guy stirred, I knew he wasn't dead, and I knew he wasn't a mouse. I placed him in an old bird cage from my Grampy's attic and nursed the odd creature back to health, fully intending to release him to freedom once he was ready. Long story short: he never was ready for the wild. I tried several times, but the orphaned rodent just wouldn't go. He must have decided that I was his mother. So with me he remained, nibbling happily on his treasured almonds and acorns, and keeping fit at night on his wheel. My animals were my family and they were also the reason I remained poor most of the time.

Since Peter Pan was nocturnal, he was only just beginning to stir when I threw my keys onto the kitchen counter. Peter Pan spent his time in an extra-tall cage complete with hammock, branches to climb, and two exercise wheels. Being a natural chewer, he can't be left out on his own, but he's extremely affectionate, so loves to be carried around in a sweater or sweatshirt pocket when I'm home.

I inhaled the burrito and soda at the counter. Unfortunately, I was hungry enough for two burritos, so I was left feeling unsatiated. Hopefully they'd have munchies at the meeting.

In my cardboard-box size of a bedroom, I pulled out a comfy, but stylish pair of denim shorts while Uno roused himself from his cat stand in the corner and padded over, purring for a chin-rub.

Choosing a shirt was trickier. "What do you think, Uno?" I asked while giving him a scratch. "T-shirt or something a little fancier?"

"You're asking fashion advice from a feline?"

I rolled my eyes. Marmi had a habit of disappearing and reappearing without notice. Right now he was posing across my bed, one elbow crooked, head resting on fist.

I stood and pulled a good old standby from the hanger in my closet. "Fancy t-shirt." Made of equal parts cotton and polyester, the blues and greens in the watercolor-style print brought out the blue in my eyes.

Marmaduke frowned. "You shouldn't wear that one. Go with a simpler piece. Less provocative."

Provocative my tushi. It was a t-shirt for crying out loud. A t-shirt that happened to be one of his favorites. He wasn't pulling the wool over my eyes. I didn't want to call him on his motivations, however. "So I shouldn't take fashion advice from a cat, but I should from a British banker who's been dead for almost a century?"

"You cut me to the quick. My feelings are truly hurt."

Needing to change quickly to avoid being late, I pointed to the door. "Out. I need to change."

"What prevents me from watching you undress while I am invisible?"

"What prevents you is our mutual agreement and your gentlemanly manners, Mr. Dodsworth. It's what I like most about you. Don't go turning creepy on me now."

"As you wish."

After changing, I brushed my hair, touched up my makeup, brushed my teeth, flossed my teeth, gargled, and double-checked my breath. Minty fresh. No, I wasn't going to be kissing anyone, but I'd be talking, and I wouldn't want to accidentally kill someone with burrito breath. Then I threw some kibble into Uno's bowl, freshened his water, scooped a few pecans and almonds into Peter Pan's cage, grabbed my keys up from the kitchen counter and, with Marmaduke on my heels, headed out to the 'support group.'

CHAPTER FIVE

Ten minutes later I limped, dripping wet, through the automatic glass doors of the swanky new community center. The heat and humidity had somehow increased tenfold during my short drive; consequently, the walk from the parking lot to the entrance felt like a three-hour workout in a steam bath. When I left my apartment I looked cute and perky. Now I felt like a grumpy river rat and was pretty sure I looked worse.

Spotting a sign for the women's restroom, I popped in, dried my sweaty forehead with a paper towel, finger brushed my hair, and reapplied a touch of lip gloss. Re-priming complete, I stepped back to the lobby running smack into a guy who was taller than me, but obviously younger. Late teens, early twenties maybe. Concerned more about the meeting and the fact that I was probably late, I gave him a quick apology – "I'm sorry!" – and scooted around him toward the electronic message board on the wall opposite us.

"Sophie," Marmaduke said. "I believe you should know that bloke—"

Not having the time or patience for a Marmi monologue, I cut him short. "Hang on to that thought, Marmi. Let me figure out which room this meeting is in."

"But that fellow just now—"

"Not now!" I whispered harshly.

The message board flashed a list of meetings with times and room locations. The Stephens City Photo Bugs were meeting in room 101 at 6:30; Jazzed for Jazz were meeting at 6:45 in room 104; The Sunny Scrapbookers were getting together in rooms 106 and 108 at 7:00. The only other group listed, also at 7:00, was Spirited Discussion, but no room was listed. Assuming Spirited Discussion was where I wanted to be, I approached a spectacled, gray-haired lady at the information desk, who told me I could find the group in room 210, which was just to the right after I got off the elevator on the second floor. I thanked her and was about to head toward the elevator when she stopped me with a question. "What exactly do you people discuss?"

Not sure exactly how much to divulge, I hesitated. When in doubt, I find it's always easiest to answer a question with a question. "Why do you ask?"

She lowered her voice. "They're just a little interesting is all. I've seen members talking to themselves when they arrive and when they put their chairs in a circle, no one sits next to each other." Her forehead unwrinkled and her voice took on a note of sympathy. "Is it a mental health support group or something?"

I forced back a grin. "Something like that, yes."

When I poked my head into room 210, Marmaduke pouting behind me, I understood her question. The chairs were in a circle alright, and seated in them were human, ghost, human, ghost, human, ghost, human, ghost. To the confused lady at the info desk, it looked like people were talking to empty chairs. Evidently, the meeting had already started, as a red-headed, extremely freckled man was arguing with a red-headed, extremely freckled ghost that looked like it could be his father. I'm guessing... it was. They halted their dispute when they saw me. The entire room of people and ghosts turned their heads in my direction. The group went silent. Finally, a woman in a floral sundress and pink flip-flops stood. "I'm sorry, but this is a closed group—"

"No, no!" Dr. Callahan waved his hand in the air, hailing me. He also addressed the flip-flop lady. "I invited her." He practically leapt from his chair to retrieve two more from a stack near the wall.

Embarrassed by the attention, I shrugged my shoulders and tip-toed to the circle while flashing an apologetic smile to the lady in the sundress. Moonflower, who sat on his left, shot angry-dagger glances in my direction, so I was very thankful when Dr. Callahan placed the chairs on his right, asking the sweet little lady there to kindly move just enough to allow room for me and my sheer friend.

All eyes, human and spirit, were focused on Marmi and me until the chairs were in place and we were finally seated. I cleared my throat, very uncomfortable with the attention. "Please," I said, "continue with your discussion. I'm so sorry to have interrupted."

"Yes," agreed Marmi. "Do go on with the chin wagging. Nothing like a good family tussle to entertain the dull and put a spark in the weary."

"Marmi," I chastised. "Don't be rude. We're guests here."

"Rudeness was certainly not my intention. I am nothing but sincere when I say I find generational drama most captivating." He turned to address the group moderator. "I so apologize if my comment was taken as cheeky."

She did not respond.

"She probably doesn't understand the word 'cheeky,'" I said.

"More apologies," he said to her. "Rude. Disrespectful. Ill-mannered."

Still, sundress lady did not respond, but did scribble on the notebook in her lap.

Marmaduke's feathers were getting ruffled again as she continued to ignore him. "Does she understand any of those words? Is the woman completely illiterate?"

I shrugged.

The freckle-faced ghost piped up. "What's chin wagging anyway?"

"Talking," answered Marmi. "Chatting or gabbing as you Americans—"

Sundress lady had finally returned her attention to the group and plowed right over Marmaduke's newest attempt at capturing an audience.

"So, welcome to our group, and a special thanks to Dr. Callahan for inviting you. My name is Sandy. I'm the group counselor. Please, go ahead and introduce yourself. Tell us your name, your friend's name, and what brought you here today."

"Yes then, well, my name is Marmaduke Dodsworth, I once hailed from the town of Dartford in Kent, England. I made passage to America in the year of—"

The lady's eyes were hooked on mine, however. I knew she wasn't listening to a thing Marmaduke was saying, but was instead, waiting for me to answer.

"Marmi," I whispered, "I think she was talking to me."

He deflated. "What am I? Chopped liver?"

"She does that to all of us," chimed in a young lady ghost dressed in a long floral dress and bonnet as if she'd once been a pioneer on the prairie. "It's like we don't even matter."

Other ghosts nodded and murmured, obviously agreeing. Not wanting to stir up trouble, I quickly answered her question. "Sophie," I said. "I'm Sophie Rhodes, this is Marmaduke. We met in a bar."

Sandy scribbled some more. "A bar," she repeated. "How exactly did you 'meet'?" She emphasized the word with her fingers mimicking quotation marks.

"What's that she's doing with her hands? Is she speaking in sign language? Does she think I'm deaf?"

"Those are finger quotes, Marmi. Let me do the talking, okay?" I took a breath, not really sure I cared very much for the way this lady ran her support group. Her questions were a tad condescending. "Last year I was sipping on a beer at my favorite hangout and he sat down next to me. We've been friends ever since."

"Do you have any sort of romantic attachment to 'Marmi'?" More finger quotes.

"No." I shook my head. "No, no, no."

"You don't have to be so adamant as if I carry the plague. I may put on a good show, a tough exterior, a facade of fortitude, but my feelings can be harmed just as easily as yours. And I don't like this woman with her obsession for... what did you call them?"

"Finger quotes," I answered, growing more and more frustrated by the minute. "I'm sorry, Marmi, I just wanted her to understand..."

"You wanted *him* to understand, you mean." He cocked his head toward Dr. Callahan whose face reddened instantly.

Moonflower's brows furrowed deeply and her lips pursed. She crossed her arms and a red aura appeared all around her, pulsing. With one particularly strong pulse, the overhead lights flickered.

"Someone is jealous," whispered Pioneer Lady to her human companion.

The sweet little lady and her male ghost were growing more and more distressed. The sweet lady finally spoke, but not so sweetly. "Why are we spending so much time on these new people? You told me at the meeting last week that we'd talk about my problem. I want to talk about *my* problem!"

"You're a problem, alright," mumbled her friend.

"Shut up, Stan. You had your chance to talk when you were alive."

"Says who? Says you? Edna, you don't let anyone–"

"Don't let anyone *what*, Stan?"

"Finish a sent—"

"See what I have to put up with?" Edna shouted. "Constant interruptions. I can't hear myself think."

"Think? You actually think? With all of your yammering—"

"Of course I think. I would have had a college degree if I hadn't married you." She shook her head. "You marry a man and think he's going to take care of you, but no! You're suddenly the new mother in their life. Doing their laundry, fixing their meals, doing their dishes, cleaning their house. And they don't even leave you alone when they die!" She turned to me. "You think that doctor is so handsome now? Think he might be husband material?" She wagged a finger of warning at me. "Run now and don't look back, Missy! You don't know how lucky you are."

The room went uncomfortably silent for a minute while my cheeks flushed from mortification. If Marmaduke wasn't already dead, I'd be ready to kill him. Out of the corner of my eye I saw Dr. Callahan fight back a grin.

"Yes, well, thank you for that bit of advice, Edna." Sandy flashed her a brief and noticeably insincere smile. "I appreciate your input. And your problem is duly noted. We'll continue to address your issues with 'Bob' as these sessions continue. So far I think you've made terrific—"

"Stan," Edna interjected before the woman was done speaking.

Sandy had armed herself with a stack of papers and stood, apparently to start handing them around the circle. "I'm sorry?"

"Stan. My husband's name is Stan. You called him Bob."

"She did that last week too," Stan muttered. "Stan. Bob. How do you get those two names—"

"Honestly," said Edna, rolling her eyes, "do you ever stop talking?"

I think Stan made a retort that was interrupted, but I had tuned them out in favor of reading the questionnaire given to me by our group's 'leader.' It started out simply enough: Name, address, date of birth. But after that, the inquest got a little suspicious. What do you call your 'spirit' or 'ghost'? Do others see or 'talk' to your ghost? Have you ever been diagnosed with a mental illness or disorder? If yes, please describe in detail along with date of diagnosis and physician's name. Are you currently taking any medications? If yes, please list along with name of prescribing physician. Please list any traumatic events in your life that might have led to the 'appearance' of the psychic phenomenon you are currently experiencing. Have you ever had any bouts with depression?

I supposed these were logical questions to ask a person who claimed to see ghosts, but the tone was too clinical for me and I noticed a definite lack of empathy. Others around the circle were looking for pens or already filling out the form. Not me. I wanted some answers of my own.

"Excuse me," I said as Sandy returned to her seat. "Since I came in a little late, I completely missed your role here."

She clasped her hands in her lap and spoke in a practiced and deliberate tone as though soothing a young child. "I'm sorry. I thought I introduced myself. I'm Sandy, the group counselor."

"You did say that, but that term, group counselor, is a little vague. What is the purpose of this group, exactly?"

"Your friend didn't tell you?"

"He did," I said, "But I'm asking you."

Her body tensed and what little smile she'd managed to maintain, faded. She rifled through some papers in her notebook and plucked one out. She read directly from the page as if she were a customer service person on the phone, dictating from one of her many scripts for handling grouchy patrons. "A Spirited Discussion is a support group for people sensitive to psychic phenomenon, particularly those visited regularly by the same ghost, spirit, demon, etc. Specifically, we will encourage interaction between human and non-human entities as well as facilitate the resolution of problems arising from such relationships."

"That sounds very helpful," I said. "As the counselor, then, you do the facilitating?"

"Very helpful indeed. And so far, this is a wonderful group. I look forward to making many inroads."

The fact that she didn't answer my question directly wasn't lost on me. I played a hunch. "What is Marmi wearing?"

She blinked, once, twice, three times. "Pardon me?"

"What am I 'wearing'?" Marmaduke made fun of Sandy's finger quotes and if my guess was correct, she didn't hear or see his sarcasm.

I motioned to the people and ghosts in the circle. "How can you facilitate any resolution between these couples if you can't see half of them?"

Sandy blinked more rapidly, evidently not expecting a challenge. "Resolution between couples?" she finally managed to sputter.

Dr. Callahan extracted his tablet from a case and started typing. "What did you say your credentials were again?"

Relief eased the lines on her face. "Dr. Sandra J. Barnes, MD, PhD. My degrees are from Harvard, Princeton, and Cornell."

He clicked away on his tablet while I pressed onward, since I didn't hear any mention of real-life experience with ghosts. "Have you ever talked to a ghost yourself?"

"I'm not sure how that is relevant..."

"It's entirely relevant," I said. "How can you help me with my ghost problems if you've never talked to one yourself?"

Marmaduke seemed hurt. "We have problems?"

"No," I said. "We don't, but these people do."

"Dr. Sandra J. Barnes," Dr. Callahan read out loud from his tablet. "Psychiatrist specializing in the narcissistic and personality disorder theory of patients exhibiting manifestations of imagined paranormal or psychic activity."

"Narcissistic?" complained red-freckled man.

"Imagined?" howled Stan.

Dr. Sandra Barnes was visibly shaken. "I don't think we should focus on those words specifically..."

"The woman is a 'fake,' an 'imposter,' and a 'swindler,'" Marmi was having a grand old time finger-quoting his many biting synonyms. "How do you like them words, Madame PhD?"

"She can't hear you, Marmi," I reminded him.

"Shall we leave this establishment, Sophie?" he asked.

"I am so sorry," Dr. Callahan whispered in my ear. "I should have checked this out better before recommending it to you."

Without thinking, I placed a comforting hand on his. "Don't worry about it," I said, while noticing again the pleasant smell of him.

The room was abuzz with chatter between humans and their ghosts, as well as between human and human and ghost and ghost. None of them were talking to 'Sandy', who looked desperate to figure out just where she'd lost control.

Older red-freckled ghost stood and pointed to Marmaduke. "I'm with the pompous British guy, let's get out of here before we wind up in one of her 'studies.' I'm not imagined and my son isn't crazy!"

People and ghosts murmured in agreement while making a mass exodus to the lobby. There, pioneer lady ghost stopped, a sense of despair on her face. "I had such high hopes," she said.

"Me too," said Edna.

Red-freckled son looked a little sad too. "I just wanted to be with people like me – people who understood me."

Dr. Callahan patted him on the back. "Know what you mean. Know what you mean."

"Maybe we could form our own group – you know, informal like," offered the woman with Pioneer Lady. "Meet at a coffee shop once a week or something."

"I don't like coffee," said Stan.

"That won't be a problem since you can't drink it then, will it?" sniffed Edna. "Don't listen to him, we'll be there. Just say where."

The idea was a good one, but meeting in a public place like a coffee shop presented what I considered to be some undesirable complications. The first time Stan and Edna went at it, the surrounding coffee-drinkers would only hear and see Edna yelling at an empty chair. I voiced this concern and the group agreed – coffee shop out.

"How about my office?" Dr. Callahan asked, turning to me. "After hours?"

"You're asking me? It's your office."

"Would you stick around? Next Tuesday night?"

I shrugged. Committing myself to weekly romps with a group of misfits and their spectral buddies wasn't really on the agenda, although, with few friends in town, my agenda was pretty non-existent anyway. "Sure. I can do that." I threw Marmaduke a questioning glance. "You, Marmi?"

"Do I have anywhere else to be, pray tell?"

Apparently everyone loved the idea of continuing the support group at Dr. Callahan's office, so he called out the address while people scribbled on whatever they had available. He gave them the office phone number as well.

"So, seven o'clock next Tuesday night, right?" he asked a final time. Everyone nodded, gave their thanks, and left the building far happier than they were when they exited Room 210 minutes earlier.

Stepping from the crisp, cooled air of the Stephens City Community Center to the steamy environment outside was almost as unsettling as that sneaky psychiatrist wanting to study me like a lab rat and label me mentally disordered.

"That was an... interesting evening," I said to Dr. Callahan. "Thank you for inviting me." I threw him a wave and began walking toward my car parked three rows back. "See you tomorrow."

The doctor followed me with Moonflower hovering right behind him. "Again – sorry for not doing my homework first."

"That's okay," I said feeling the awkwardness of the moment as I tried to say goodbye, despite the fact that we were both walking in the same direction. "Where are you parked?"

He pointed. "Over there. Silver Chevy."

I laughed, relieved. "I parked right next to you."

"Isn't that convenient?" mumbled Moonflower. The air was already thick with humidity, but I swear I felt a surge of electricity zip through my nerves immediately after her snide comment.

When we reached our cars, he stopped. He held his tablet at his side in his left hand and jiggled a set of keys in his right. He'd changed from his business attire into a nicely pressed pair of khakis and blue polo shirt. The look was a little preppy, but I liked it. "So," he said, seeming like he'd prefer to hang around. "What a day, huh?"

"Yeah, what a day," I nodded, leaning against my car. I didn't want to be rude. If he wanted to talk for a few minutes before parting ways, I'd oblige.

"So, I have to know," he said, jingling his keys and grinning slightly. "How exactly do you meet a ghost in a bar? Was he trying to pick you up?"

I laughed. "I think he felt sorry for me. It was... well, it was a bad night for me."

"I'm sorry. Forget I asked. I didn't mean to be nosy."

"No, don't be sorry. I understand. It's not every day that someone says they met a ghost in a bar."

"It's not every day that someone says they met a ghost at all."

"True enough." I laughed. "It was..." I took a moment to count back. "I guess about seven months ago. I was supposed to meet my boyfriend there. We were going to get a drink then head out to the movies. He never showed. I couldn't reach him on his cell phone. He'd stood me up before and blamed it on the job – he's a cop – but since I also worked at the station, I knew better. So, to make a long story longer, after two beers and many tears, Marmi was there in the chair next to me."

"And you knew he was a ghost right away?"

"Are you kidding me? I thought he was a lonely Brit with really bad fashion sense. The next morning though, when he appeared out of thin air while I was eating my cereal – that's when I knew I'd been adopted by a ghost. I wouldn't say my... acceptance of the fact was exactly smooth. There was some screaming first." I wrinkled my nose. "Quite a bit of screaming. Before the epiphany."

He laughed. "You're funny." He jingled his keys some more. "So why you? Have you ever asked him why he went home with you?"

Marmi materialized, his arms crossed. "She was special." He was very matter-of-fact and used less words than usual.

Dr. Callahan tipped his head and smiled. He responded to Marmaduke, but held my gaze. "I think you're right. Very special."

Blue. His eyes shone so much bluer against that turquoise shirt. Like a Caribbean ocean. And the lines that sprung up around them when he smiled. My stomach squeezed. I quickly grabbed hold of my senses and tore my eyes away from his. *Can't fall for my boss. Can't do it.* I fanned myself with my hand. "Man, it's hot out here." I dug into my purse looking for my keys. "I need to, you know, get home. Out of the heat. Where are those keys?"

I felt something wiggle on my hip.

"You mean these keys?" asked Dr. Callahan.

Mental head slap. Of course, I had clipped them onto a belt loop of my shorts – like I usually did. I blushed and as I moved my hand to unclip them, brushed his. The moment of contact was brief, but enough to cause my blush to deepen and my skin to tingle. In a good way. In a really, really good way.

"Thanks," I said. "That was silly of me."

He nodded and jiggled his keys around more briskly. "Right. I mean, no, not silly at all. I'll see you tomorrow, right?"

I scooted to my car door and unlocked it fast to escape more gawky bumbling. I was behaving like a crushing high school girl. "Right. In the morning. Have a good night."

"Hey!" He called across the car, catching my attention. "For the record, I think that boyfriend of yours was an idiot."

Suddenly, that electrical surge I had felt before returned, but this time easily, ten times stronger. I looked up in time to see Moonflower glowering behind Dr. Callahan like an angry cat ready to pounce. The hair on my arms stood on end and I was about to ask if he felt the current when a loud, deep pop shook me and caused me to flinch. Out of the corner of my eye I saw a flash of light and when I turned to the noise, saw that the streetlight behind us had blown, showering sparks onto the cars below.

"Whoa!" shouted Dr. Callahan. "What caused that?"

My hair fell and the electric sensation passed. That was my cue to get the heck out of there. I threw open my door. "Storm is coming, maybe?" I asked. "See you tomorrow!" Once safely in my car with the engine running, I questioned Marmaduke. "That was Moonflower, wasn't it?"

"That was most definitely the work of your good doctor's friend."

"Can you do that?"

"I will admit that I do not know. Would you like me to try?"

"No, no! I've had enough surprises for one day."

"Well, could I bother you with one more strange item?"

"Strange?"

"Look in your rearview mirror."

I did what he said.

"Tell me what you see," he continued.

"Cars."

"Besides the auto cars."

Behind two rows of cars was a row of hedges. In front of the hedges, a man. Well, not a man, he was probably nineteen or twenty. "You mean the guy standing in front of that hedge?" Dr. Callahan's car backed up and pulled away. My attention went from the rearview mirror to his car and I had to smile as I saw him give me a final wave as his tail lights moved off.

"Rear view mirror, Sophie, rear view mirror."

My eyes snapped back and caught sight of the teen who I suddenly recognized as the one I had collided with in the community center lobby. His hair was blondish and a little long, hanging in his eyes a bit, his clothes standard summer apparel – gray shorts and an orange t-shirt. Nothing about him seemed suspicious, except that his eyes were glued to Dr. Callahan's car as it motored out of the parking lot.

"Why am I watching this guy, Marmi?"

"I saw that young man earlier today."

"Yeah. Me too. In the lobby."

Marmaduke shook his head. "Earlier than that."

Uh oh. "You tried to warn me at the message board, didn't you?"

"Would you like to hear what I have to say at this time, or shall you once more smash my attempt to communicate the way a batsman tonks a lollipop?"

I suppressed an eye roll and pressed my temples to fend off an impending headache. "Translate, please?"

"In the game of cricket. When the man at bat wallops an easy toss by the bowler."

Cricket. Of course. Marmi loved the game. He also loved to throw me off with cricket analogies, using terms I could never understand. Presently, I sensed he was doing so as retribution for dismissing him earlier. Fair enough. Probably not a nice way to treat a ghost who thinks I'm special. "Okay," I surrendered. "I'm sorry for tonking your lollipop. Without further ado, would you tell me where you saw him earlier?" I asked the question, but the kid's attention on Dr. Callahan's car gave me a good idea.

"Outside your doctor's office. He meandered along the cement walk three or four times, glancing through the windows with each pass."

"You think he's following Dr. Callahan?"

"It would appear that way."

CHAPTER SIX

Despite the fact that my apartment building supposedly had air conditioning, it never seemed to function well enough to keep my unit comfortably cool. At best, when running, it fended off most of the humidity. For some reason, the heat bothered me even more that night – sleeping became a toss and turn affair. Lots of pillow plumping, frustrated sighing, and brief interludes of light, restless dreaming. By five a.m., I gave up the ghost, pun intended, and started my day with a shower and a giant glass of ice cold, caffeine-laced soda.

My hours, per our agreement, were nine-thirty to six-fifteen, but I decided to arrive an hour early since I was awake and had nothing better to do. I figured I could spend the extra time educating myself on Dr. Callahan's brand of optometry so I could sound semi-intelligent on the phone when people called to inquire.

When I arrived, I was surprised to see an unmarked police car in the lot and a uniformed man cupping his hand against the glass panes of Dr. Callahan's front door, peeking inside. Even from the side, the policeman's dark, wavy hair and macho-confident stance were unmistakable. Our lawman visitor was my ex-boyfriend, Shane Daniels. My bad night was transforming into a tragic day. Half of me considered sneaking slowly and stealthily back into my car, and then tearing off frantically in search of a large supply of chocolate and a dark room to gorge myself. The other half of me thought that was a good idea as well. Thank goodness for Marmaduke. He had better sense than either of my halves.

"Don't you dare run away from that brute, Sophie," he said, appearing at my side and reading my mind all at the same time. "He doesn't deserve to walk on the same ground as you, much less have the power to scare you away. Don't grant him the satisfaction."

"But if he doesn't see me, he won't know he was satisfied."

"Are you a coward or a hero in your own life?"

"Since when did you take up motivational speaking?"

"I'm not sure I understand your meaning."

"Never mind." I took a deep breath. "You're right. I can do this." I took a second deep breath. "Let me center myself..." I closed my eyes and while taking a third, deep (probably too deep) cleansing breath, Shane must have caught sight of me.

"Sophie?"

I opened my eyes and felt the ground sway. Too many deep breaths had made me dizzy. "Shane. Hey." I giggled nervously which made me furious with myself. Immediately, I took a more serious tone. "Is there a reason you're spying on my place of employment?"

He took several steps in my direction. "I'm on duty, Soph. It's hardly spying." He pointed back to the office. "You work there now?"

"Strong, Sophie," encouraged Marmi as Shane moved even closer. "Be strong."

My feet felt heavy as ship anchors, unable to move. "I do." I nodded vigorously. "Excellent job. Wonderful employer. I'm very happy there."

"How long?"

Should have kept my mouth shut. Now I had to a) answer that question honestly and sound ridiculous since one day was hardly enough time to be boasting of success on the job; b) lie and make myself look good; or c) evade brilliantly. I decided to give brilliance a try. "Long enough."

"Masterful dodge, my friend!" shouted Marmaduke, clapping. "Bravo."

The urge to bow was intense, but I resisted. I also suppressed the Cheshire grin that desperately wanted to erupt on my face. "If you're on duty," I continued, buoyed by my attack of quick-wittedness, "what's your business here?" I unstuck my anchor-weighted feet, maneuvered around Shane, onto the sidewalk, to the door, and then slipped the key into the lock. The entire move was made with such finesse that I made James Bond look like a klutz. I was on a dauntless roll and felt pretty darned proud of myself.

When I opened the door and stepped in, however, the security alarm began its warning beep, shattering my bravura. My mind blanked on the security code. It had seemed easy enough to remember the day before when Dr. Callahan gave it to me. So easy, in fact, that I neglected to actually write it down. Was it 4 0 8 8? Or 8 4 8 0? There was definitely a 4 and an 8, I knew that. A zero too. What was I missing? In a fit, I threw my purse to the floor, fully aware of Shane standing next to me, staring me down while I wracked my brain for the correct sequence of numbers.

Marmaduke sensed my memory loss. "Zero, four, two, eight," he said.

That was it. I'd forgotten the two. "Thank you," I mumbled while punching in the numbers on the alarm keypad. The unit double beeped, accepting the correct code, and I slammed the cover shut, only to realize Shane was giving me a queer look.

"Are you talking to ghosts again, Soph?"

I picked up my purse, regained my composure and stepped around behind the desk. "I told you, that was just a joke, Shane. Would you let it go?" Many months earlier, in my naiveté, believing Shane to be mature, nurturing, and open-minded, I had confided my secret to him, expecting support. Why I ever thought Shane was any of those things is beyond me, since I met Marmaduke on a night when Shane had stood me up. Forget naiveté, it was just plain stupidity. "By the way," I said, deciding to fight fire with fire, "How's Lame-y?"

"That's not nice. You're a better person than that."

"Sorry. I forgot my manners. How's Cockamamy?"

"Amy is fine." He scanned his surroundings. "So this guy puts braces on kids' teeth?"

"Optometrist you idiot. He's an optometrist, not an orthodontist. Dr. Callahan is an eye doctor."

"We got a report that someone has been casing your eye doctor's office. That's why I'm here."

That caught my attention. "Really? Who called it in?"

"An accountant upstairs. Says she arrived around seven-forty-five this morning to find a white male, about five-ten, light brown hair, possibly early twenties, trying to break into this unit. When she shouted at him, he ran off." He watched my reaction for a beat before continuing. "You see anyone around here by that description?"

Technically, I had not seen that kid hanging around the office yesterday, Marmaduke had. Truthfully, I had seen him the night before, possibly following Dr. Callahan, which was really, very creepy. The question was, should I tell Shane? Telling him that I had been with Dr. Callahan after business hours could make him very jealous. Did I want to make him jealous? As much as I hated him, there was something way-too animal that attracted me to him, so the desire to raise the green-eye monster was strong. On the other hand, if I mentioned the evening rendezvous, would the true purpose of our meeting come to light? I sure didn't need to fuel Shane's Sophie-sees-ghosts machinery. Finally, I opted for the easy way out.

"No," I said. "Haven't seen anyone matching that description around here, but I feel safe knowing Stephens City's best is watching out for me. I'll definitely keep my eyes peeled and let you know if I do. Thanks for stopping by. That door is the way out." My hand motioned him to get a move on. "I need to get to work, please."

"Be sure to alert your employer."

"Will do. Bye-bye now." I plopped my butt in the rolling chair and focused my attention on the laptop computer on the desk, powering it on.

"Good to see you again, Soph."

I wouldn't take my eyes off the still blank monitor. "Can't say the same."

When the door clicked shut, I let out a releasing sigh. In times of stress, I hold back my breath – I don't actually stop breathing, but the shallow, short breaths lead to a lack of oxygen that only adds to my frazzled state of mind. It was good to have Shane out of the office, only now I was plagued with concern for Dr. Callahan.

Marmaduke stood near the door glaring through the glass panes. "If only these fists were made of skin and bone – I'd punch that bloke from here to Kalamazoo."

"That would be unfair to Kalamazoonians." I rubbed my temples and then set myself to getting some work done.

Dr. Callahan arrived a few minutes before ten, a tight frown on his face and an even gloomier looking Moonflower floating above him. Either he'd had trouble sleeping as well or Moonflower was giving him trouble. Or possibly the latter causing the former.

His nod was terse. "Morning, Sophie." With a laptop case flung over his shoulder, he made a beeline for his examining room.

"I made you a pot of coffee," I said sweetly.

He stopped abruptly and his shoulders relaxed. "Really? You didn't have to do that."

"I know, but I was here, so why not. You do drink coffee, right? I saw the pot and the can in the kitchenette."

He nodded. "Definitely. Did you make yourself a cup?"

I shook my head. "Not a coffee drinker. Caffeine-rich soda, yes, but not coffee."

"Well, thank you. I appreciate it."

He disappeared for a few minutes, then reappeared, a little less rigid, holding a cup of my brew by the handle. He hovered around the front desk, sipping. "What does my day look like?" He swatted at Moonflower, who flitted around his head.

"You have an exam at eleven, one at noon, then nothing until three-thirty when you have three back-to-back therapy sessions. And, uh, before I forget..." Ugh. I hated asking about money, but I needed some fast. "I know I just started, and..." Spit it out, I said to myself, just spit it out. "Paycheck. I was wondering when you write paychecks."

"When do you need one?"

"Friday would be, like, really wonderful." Ah geez. Nothing better to prove your worth as an employee than to talk like a Valley Girl.

"Sure. No problem. I'll pay you the end of each week. That's how I worked it with the others."

"There's one other thing."

"What's that?"

"A, uh, police officer was here this morning when I arrived." I purposely left out the part about the policeman being the ex-boyfriend I'd mentioned the night before. Way too much information. "He said that the accountant upstairs witnessed someone trying to break into this office early this morning."

His blue eyes darkened. He'd just been going for a sip from his mug when I laid that whopper on him. "Someone who? Did they trip the alarm?"

"No. Everything is fine. She scared him away. He was a kid – probably nineteen or twenty. Dirty blond hair. Around five foot ten, or five foot eleven." I watched his face for signs of recognition. "Does any of that sound familiar? Maybe you've seen someone like that around here before?"

He shook his head. "No. I'd better call the condo association and make sure they increase security."

"I don't want to alarm you, but..."

"When you start out with the word alarm, it's very alarming."

"It may not be anything, but Marmaduke and I saw a kid who looked very much like that last night at the community center. And Marmaduke saw the same guy walking back and forth in front of this office earlier yesterday."

"That certainly sounds like something to me. I'm definitely calling the condo association now." He swatted again as Moonflower's activity grew more and more invasive. Finally, he plunked his cup on the desktop and turned around and looked up at her, his face stern. "Would you please leave me alone! Can't you see I have work to do?" He shook his fists in the air, as if that would shoo her away. With a distraught look on her filmy face, she went instantly invisible.

"Giving you a little trouble, is she?"

"She's worse than usual. She kept me awake all night crying and moaning. And she clings to me like saran wrap. Maybe you could have a talk with her?"

I cringed. "Not sure that's a good idea. I might be the problem."

"You think so?"

"She seems to have a jealous streak. Or at least she doesn't like me."

"Jealous?"

"Some women are like that. You know, jealous of other women in general."

"Great. Not only do I attract a ghost, but I have to attract a troubled one during one of the worst times of my life."

"What's wrong with your life?"

"Never mind. That's a little overdramatic. You know, opening this new office on my own. And now, someone trying to break in."

"Well, that's why I'm here, Dr. Callahan. To make all of that easier for you. I'll call the condo association for you. Their number is in the rolodex."

He rolled his eyes. "I hate that."

"What?"

"Dr. Callahan. You can't call me Cal?"

"I thought we agreed I should call you Dr. Callahan around the office."

"In front of patients. Do you see any patients?"

"I thought doctors liked that –to be called Doctor. Isn't that why you became one?"

"No."

"I'm sorry, that was just meant to be a joke. It came out wrong."

"That's okay. No offense taken."

"Why did you?"

"What?"

"Become an eye doctor?"

"My sister. Emily."

"She wanted you to be an eye doctor?"

"Not just any kind of eye doctor – a developmental optometrist. She thought I should do vision therapy."

"Why?"

"She had a tough time growing up. Learning was always easy for me. Not her. Just the opposite. Reading was a problem. It came slow for her, and then, even when she learned to read, she'd get headaches. She'd throw up. My parents sent her to a bunch of different doctors the school recommended, but nothing worked. They just wanted to label her as a basket case and give her drugs. None of which helped her learn, by the way, and actually made matters worse because of the side effects." He broke for a sip from his cup. "So finally," he continued, "our eye doctor at the time sent her to a specialist – a developmental optometrist. She did vision therapy with him, and after a year, was reading without headaches or nausea, and after another year was finally catching up to grade level with her friends. I was in college at the time and trying to decide on a career path to follow and she told me that if I really wanted to make a difference in the world for even one person, I should do vision therapy. I liked that idea." He sipped from his cup. "And here I am. Many years and many college loans later."

I leaned back in my chair, very impressed. A lot of people talk about choosing a career that will make a difference, but not everyone does it. "I feel awful that I even tried to make a joke about that. What a great story." The warmth in his voice when he told the story spoke volumes about his love for his sister, too. I threw him a teasing grin. "Does she like to take credit for the man you've become?"

His jaw clenched and from the lag in his response, I knew his answer wouldn't be equally quippy. "She's, um..." He cleared his throat. "She's not with us anymore. She was killed in a car crash seven years ago."

I lowered my eyes, feeling horrible for my flippancy.

"My many condolences, lad," said Marmaduke, appearing next to him. "I lost a sister. It's a terrible, terrible loss to bear."

I had no words and a sticky, awkward silence hung in the air while I scrambled to say something of substance. Saying 'I'm sorry,' to a person who has lost a loved one never felt like enough to me. Yet, it was all I could come up with. "I am really, really so sorry."

He slapped his hands on the counter and pasted a semi-smile on his face. "Thank you, but I'm the one who should be sorry for putting a downer on the morning. We've got work to do, right? Patients to see. Those two patients this morning – do you have their files for me to review before they arrive?"

I nodded and reached for a file to hand him. "One. The other is a new patient."

"Good. We like new patients, don't we?" He took the one file, his cup of coffee, and retreated to his exam room.

"He really is a good bloke, that doctor," said Marmaduke, shaking his head in sympathy.

"I know. And how sad is that about his sister?"

"Sad, as you say. Sad," agreed Marmi.

Then we sat, not speaking, while I quietly considered Dr. Callahan's cause. He'd chosen a profession that gave him a purpose. That, I thought, was not only cool, it was smart.

CHAPTER SEVEN

I did as I promised and called the condo association. The manager said she hadn't had any other reports of a young white male casing the office park, but she would put in a call to the security company and ask them to do extra rounds and be on alert.

Later, after he'd finished up with his second patient of the day, Dr. Callahan took off, car keys in his hands. "I'm heading out to grab my lunch and some light bulbs from the store. Can I get you anything?"

"No thanks, I brought my lunch."

I pulled my measly little egg salad sandwich out of my purse, filled a coffee cup with water, and sat back down at the computer with a project in mind. Obviously, Dr. Callahan needed more patients, and it seemed, based on what research I'd done on vision therapy and learning problems, that there were a great many patients that needed him. Figuring I could do some good and help secure my new job, I began the work on a plan to bring them together.

Four bites into my sandwich and three minutes of work on my project, the door opened. Looking up from my computer, I was surprised to see Dory Ellison burdened by a cellophane wrapped gift basket so large it overflowed her arms and concealed most of her upper body. In fact, I only knew it was Dory because of the flaming red manicured nails and an oddly meek Ronald Ellison who stood beside her.

"My, my," said Marmaduke, "what do we have here?"

My thought exactly.

Dory tottered toward me and set the mammoth offering onto the desk. She let out a sigh of relief and peeked around the package. "Hello again! Is Dr. Callahan in?"

"He stepped out."

"For long?"

"I'm not sure. He said he was getting lunch and light bulbs. Can I help you?"

"I—" she stopped short and corrected herself. "We were just stopping by to say thank you for saving my dear Ronald's life."

Dear Ronald bobbed his head a couple of times. "We brought a gift basket."

"Yes, I see," I said, standing to push it to the far side of the desk so I could see them better. "It's . . . big." I smiled at Mr. Ellison, noticing how healthy he appeared for someone who had just died the day before. Timid, but healthy. He hadn't seemed nearly as mousy as a ghost. "How are you feeling?" I asked hesitantly, surprised he was up and walking around.

Ronald opened his mouth to speak, but Dory bowled him over with her own response. "Not a thing wrong with him. Can you believe it? The doctors at the hospital were speechless. Speechless."

"What happened? I mean, do they know what caused you to..."

"Die?" asked Ronald, completing my thought. He shook his head. "No."

"They think he had some sort of cardiac episode, but so far he shows no signs of heart distress or blockages." She patted him on the back like she was patting a dog on the head.

"He sees his cardiologist next week and they'll run some more tests to be sure, but I am just so grateful to Dr. Callahan. If he hadn't performed that CPR, I don't think I'd have my Ronny with me today."

Dory's Ronny didn't seem as joyous, but he did offer his own thanks. "Yes. So grateful."

I was curious if he had any memory of being outside of his body. I just had to inquire. "Do you remember anything about yesterday? You know, a pain, or anything?" I couldn't exactly ask him directly if he remembered being a ghost for thirty minutes, so I had to take a more circuitous route.

"No pain." He shook his head. "Don't even remember going into that room you found me in. The last thing I remember was packing up some paperwork to take with me. I had a house to show."

"And then... nothing?" I pressed.

I swear I saw Ronald glance in Marmaduke's direction while he spent a few seconds working up an answer. "Eh. Don't think so." He shook his head again. "Nope."

Dory patted his hand. "We were really hoping to give this to Dr. Callahan with our personal message of gratitude, but at least tell him we stopped by and we'll come around again."

"Okay, I will."

They looked ready to leave when Marmaduke nudged me. Figuratively. "Ask them about the girl."

For a minute I didn't understand his meaning.

"The girl who died in this office."

Right. Moonflower. Possibly. I stopped them before they'd turned their backs to me. "I was wondering if you could tell me a little about the previous owner of this unit?"

Ronald spun back around, quick on his feet to respond. "She died a year ago, last... September I think it was."

Dory seemed confused by what she obviously considered a non-sequitur.

"Wasn't it September, Dory?" he asked.

Marmaduke narrowed his eyes. "You didn't ask him about the girl. You asked him about the owner. That bloke heard me talking to you!"

He sure did. And that's why Dory was thrown for a loop.

She shook her head, looking at him like he'd lost more than a marble or two. "The owner," she said to me, thinking she was covering for her silly husband, "was a very quiet Indian man. Mr. Bhandari. He owned an insurance business. Ran it out of this office. What Ronald is talking about – well, it was just plain tragic. We really don't know much about what happened except that she died right here." She lowered her voice as if she needed to keep the information from someone. "Probably right where we're standing now."

"How?"

"No one knows. Like I said, he was a quiet man. Kept to himself. Your neighbor, the travel agent," she pointed to my right, "That's Mrs. Wilkins. She claims she heard them fighting, then she heard Mr. Bhandari scream. A few minutes later the police and medics arrived, but there was nothing they could do. By the end of the year, he'd put the condo on the market. I was a little disappointed he didn't ask us to list it."

"Did you know his daughter's name, the girl who died?"

Ronald stepped in. "Jina. She wasn't aloof like her father. She came to our office once asking if we needed any summer hires."

"We didn't." Dory sniffed.

"She needed the work. She was a nice girl. And she got a lot of our filing done." Ronald's face grew a little rigid and he looked right at Marmaduke before asking me, "Why are you so interested?"

"Because she's floating around here like The Ghost of Christmas Dread, that's why," said Marmaduke.

Ronald stiffened.

"I was just curious," I said. "I heard some people talking. You know how people talk."

"Yes, they do," agreed Dory. "Well, let's go, Ronny, we have clients to see."

She pushed him out the door.

"That girl's name was Jina. Doesn't sound anything like Moonflower. You think it's the same girl?"

He shrugged. "We could ask her."

I wasn't sure I wanted to get into any long conversations with a ghost that didn't seem nearly as nice as the person Ronald Ellison had described, but I thought about it. I also thought about approaching Shane on the subject. If he was the responding police officer that day, he could probably give me more than the Ellisons since Mr. Bhandari had remained so tight-lipped. Playing Shane for information wasn't my idea of fun, so I tucked it away in the recesses of my mind for future consideration and set back to work creating business for my employer.

When Dr. Callahan returned with McDonald's and a bag of light bulbs, he was surprised by the substantial token left by the Ellisons. He cut off the ribbon and began inspecting the contents: cinnamon flavored coffee beans, a small grinder, candied almonds, sesame crackers, wheat crackers, pepper jack cheese, a cheddar cheese roll, a giant milk chocolate candy bar, trail mix, an assortment of herbal teas, a baby-sized loaf of rye bread, and a salami. Except for the coffee, it all looked wonderfully tasty.

Skipping breakfast and ingesting a meager egg salad sandwich for lunch had made for a very hungry Sophie. With payday still two days off and my refrigerator emptier than a pessimist's glass, the very sight of it all made my mouth water. An envelope clung to the side of the cellophane. I pulled it free and handed it to Dr. Callahan.

He read from the card inside: "Words and gift baskets alone cannot express our deepest and sincerest gratitude. But please, enjoy a night at Winston's on us." He held up a gift certificate. "One hundred dollars. They really shouldn't have. I feel terrible taking this when I did what anyone would have done."

"I wouldn't feel terrible. You did a good thing," I said, even though I knew Ronald really brought himself around all on his own. Winston's though. Wow. That was one fancy, classy, and very expensive restaurant. I'd never been there myself, but a co-worker at the police department had, and she told me all about it. The waiters pulled your chair out for you and everything. A hundred dollars was probably a usual tab for a two-person dinner at that place.

"You called 911," he said. Then suddenly he was putting everything back into the basket, including the gift certificate, and pushing it at me. "You take it. You probably need this more than me."

The desire to shout, "Yes I do!" and snatching the thing, was strong, but I shoved the basket back anyway. "No. They brought this for you. Besides, I don't like coffee, remember?"

We played a rousing round of You Take It No You Take it until finally he stopped, took the coffee, coffee grinder, and gift certificate out. "Fine. Here's the deal. I take the coffee, you take everything else – cheese and chocolate don't like me anyway – and we both use the gift certificate." He anticipated my protest, holding up a hand. "Not a date, a business dinner. We'll discuss business."

"At Winston's?"

"Absolutely. I'll bring a steno pad and take notes. Very official. Very business like."

I thought about it. Actually, I only played like I was thinking about it so I wouldn't look so desperate for the food. After an appropriate number of seconds, I agreed, thankful to have cheese, crackers, and salami dinner already planned.

"Good," he said with that cute, crooked smile of his. "Good." As he walked by me, I was way too aware of his scent again. Definitely cologne, I decided. Really, really nice cologne.

The rest of the day was slow, but steady. Moonflower had been invisible for most of it, or at least to me. During Dr. Callahan's last therapy appointment though, a phone call came in from a parent who said she thought her daughter had pink-eye, but wasn't sure. So new to the whole receptionist-thing, I wasn't quite sure what to do. I decided to put her on hold and ask the man himself. Knocking lightly and hoping he wouldn't be mad at the interruption, I held my breath.

"Come in," I heard him say.

I opened the door just enough to poke my head in and see Dr. Callahan seated across a rectangular table from Kaylee, his eight-year old patient. She wore a pair of funky looking glasses – one lens was green, the other was red – and she was poking at something on the table with a pick-up stick. Unfortunately, Moonflower was there as well, hovering beside Dr. Callahan. All three of them stopped to look up at me.

"I'm sorry to bother you, but Mrs. Wallace is on the phone. She thinks her daughter has pink eye, but isn't sure. Did you want to talk to her?"

Dr. Callahan smiled and well, I just couldn't help but smile back. It was a really cute, crooked smile after all. Our exchange was not appreciated by Moonflower. An electrical sensation overwhelmed me again, my hair standing on end. This was even stronger than the night before, and I knew Dr. Callahan and Kaylee felt it too by the alarm on their faces.

"Um, tell her..."

The charge strengthened, the lights pulsed, then Moonflower let out a banshee wail that resonated and echoed down the hall. Kaylee covered her ears, and her mother yelled from the waiting room, "What was that?"

Poor little Kaylee screamed as a light above her dimmed, grew brighter, then burst with a pop. She tore off the funny looking glasses and screamed all the way to her mother, begging to leave and never come back to "this scary office."

CHAPTER EIGHT

I arrived at the office early again the next day and cringed when I listened to the messages on voicemail. Kaylee's mother was canceling appointments for the next two weeks. The little girl was absolutely adamant that she never wanted to return to "that scary place," but her mother was hopeful that Kaylee would forget the event after a couple of weeks' time and they could return for therapy. I erased Kaylee from the book for the two weeks and wrote the note for Dr. Callahan, who surely wouldn't be happy. Unfortunately, he arrived unhappy, but less one gloomy ghost. I decided to hold back the note until his mood improved, but just had to ask about Moonflower since she was so obviously absent.

"So, you're alone this morning?"

"She's probably around. Give her a minute, I'm sure, and she'll show up to ruin my day. Any messages?"

"Nothing urgent." I thought some good news might cheer him up. "You have two new patients today – brothers."

He didn't crack a smile, but the tension in his shoulders relaxed. "That's good."

I handed him a list of his patients for the day. "What's this?"

"Your schedule – you can keep it with you in your exam room."

Finally he smiled. "Thanks. Very organized. And helpful. Look, an exam at ten. I'd better get ready. Do you have Mrs. Spodowski's file?"

"In your room already."

His smile broadened and he moved down the hall with a little more bounce in his step than when he'd entered just minutes earlier.

When the door opened, I looked over the desk, expecting to see a somewhat early Mrs. Spodowski, but instead was confronted by a young girl. She appeared to be in her late teens, maybe sixteen or seventeen with brownish, wavy hair that hung just below her shoulders. She wore a faded and tattered Army green jacket that was about three sizes too large for her, and looked entirely out of place considering the near triple digit heat index outside. Under the jacket was a striped tank.

"Can I help you?" I asked, thinking she had probably wandered into the wrong office.

"I..." She scanned the room, then brought her eyes back to mine, but only for a nanosecond. She was scanning the room again when she finished her sentence finally. "... need an eye exam. I think I need glasses."

The girl's gaze darted here and there, but she wouldn't focus her attention on me. As if eye contact might harm her in some way.

"I could probably put you in for an exam with Dr. Callahan," I started cautiously, "but we don't have eyeglasses here. You'd need to get them somewhere else. Dr. Callahan actually specializes—"

"That'd be okay." She drummed her fingers on the counter, bounced a little, and finally settled her eyes on a filing cabinet behind me. "Probably. Maybe."

Not sure what I was dealing with, I decided to delve into the age issue indirectly. "Possibly your mom or dad would like to come in or call, to make this appointment—"

Finally, eye contact. "Never mind. It's good." As quickly as she'd appeared, she was gone, like Speedy Gonzales. I actually think some papers on the desk ruffled in the breeze left behind.

Jumping from my desk quickly, I bounded to the door and peered out, hoping to catch a glimpse of her and which direction she'd gone. It didn't take me long to spot her far off next to a tree, talking closely with none other than the sandy-haired boy from the night at the community center. My red flag alert rose to danger. Were they thieves, casing Dr. Callahan's office? Maybe they thought there were valuable eyeglass frames to steal? I threw open the door, intent on finding out what they were up to, but they saw me advancing and tore off in opposite directions. At that very moment, an elderly woman made a slow approach toward our door, and suspecting she was our patient, Mrs. Spodowski, I fell back to do my job. I knew though, that I'd have to tell Dr. Callahan now about the boy and his partner. Whatever they were up to, thievery or something else, it obviously involved him.

After Dr. Callahan took Mrs. Spodowski back for her exam, I used the quiet time without ringing phones to go through drawers and organize. A pair of identical tiny keys were thrown haplessly in a glass bowl with a wad of rubber bands, paper clips, and thumbtacks. Nearly pricking myself on the thumbtacks, I pulled out the keys joined on a small ring. They looked like my mailbox keys at the apartment.

Realizing I had never seen mail since starting, and having not noticed Dr. Callahan returning with any himself, I decided to look around the condo complex for a mailbox. Not only did

I find the mailbox, I found it stuffed to the gills. As I carried the heavy load back to the office, I caught a glimpse of Moonflower pouting in the shade-giving dogwood tree, closely following my movement. Before I could open the door, she disappeared from her perch and appeared next to me, her face right in mine. "You can go now," she said. "We don't need you."

"Funny," I countered, "I was thinking the same thing." I decided to play a hunch and see how she reacted. "What exactly is your problem, Jina?"

For just a moment, after I uttered the name, she flickered off, then on again, as if she were an image on a television that lost power briefly. I also detected a minor shift in her expression, but so minor, I didn't know if I should dismiss it, or think it was a sign that she was in fact, Jina Bhandari. The door opened, startling me, and Dr. Callahan stuck his head out. "Oh! You got the mail. Thank you. I thought I'd lost the key." He tipped his head back toward the desk. "I need you to check Mrs. Spodowski out. Just charge her for a follow-up – she didn't need a full exam."

I nodded and slipped past him, irritated by the fact that Moonflower had practically glued herself to Dr. Callahan again at the same time. I'd had enough of this morose phantom. Then, of course, I realized suddenly why Dr. Callahan couldn't keep a receptionist. She'd been scaring them off. A few, or even all of them, probably didn't even know why. The problem was, after taking that call from Kaylee's mom earlier, I now knew she was also scaring off his patients.

It was just after lunch when the front door opened and two red-haired boys erupted onto the scene, instantly turning our quiet office into a den of din. Not only did they have identical hair, they had identical faces, and identical activity levels. They reminded me of rubber bouncy balls run amok. A moment later, a woman, very obviously their mother from the matching hair color and facial features, stepped in, all smiles. At least, she was all smiles for a second or two. Then she swayed, as if the floor gave out from under her. Her hands felt the air around her while her eyes widened. "Whoa," was all she said. She shook her head, then her hands, and the smile returned. She stepped up to the desk.

"Are you okay?" I wondered if she was close to fainting – possibly the heat was getting to her.

"I'm just fine." She cocked an eyebrow. "Are you okay?"

Not sure if she was cuckoo or just a little odd, I decided to move on with my receptionist duties rather than address her query. I peeked down at the appointment book. "Is this Robert and Michael?"

She acknowledged them with a smile. "They're the ones."

I handed her a clipboard. "I have two forms there. One for each of them. Once you fill them out, Dr. Callahan can get started with the examinations."

My nerves were thankful that one of the boys had settled in a chair with a book. The other, however, was rolling two toy cars around on the wall near the door. He crashed them into each other often and loudly vocalized their explosive collisions. Very loudly.

"Robert!" his mother chastised him firmly. "That is very poor manners and unacceptable behavior. If you are going to play with those toys, do it quietly on the floor."

"But I like playing with it on the wall." More crashing, more explosions.

She leaned in toward his face and spoke in a quietly calm, but no-nonsense tone. "Then I will have to teach you how to paint that wall for Dr. Callahan after you've left black marks all over it with your playing. And it won't be like the fun painting you do at school. That kind of painting will require hours of time and hard work because you will have to repair any dents first, then sand it, probably paint it several times to get it looking like new. Lots of blood, sweat, and tears, my friend." By the end of her speech, Michael had stopped his fidgeting entirely and his eyes looked ready to pop out of their sockets. She laid a hand on his shoulder. "Should we begin that difficult and rigorous training now, or would you like to just play on the floor?"

He gave that proposition about one second of thought then dropped to the floor, once again mimicking the sound of a car's engine, and I was very thankful to his mother for her keen and responsible parenting. Getting along with kids was not a skill listed on my résumé. I'd never babysat as a teenager, I'd never aspired to have a job working with children, and had next to no experience with them. That being said, I did hope to be a mother one day, but only after taking a master class or something. To avoid traumas like dropping the baby on its head or scarring the child emotionally for life by ripping those toy cars from his grubby little hands and screaming, "Stop that infernal racket now or I'll sell you to a band of pirates!"

Marmaduke, probably reading my mind, appeared next to me. "Thank goodness for small miracles and resolute mothers. That child was putting me on edge. If I had a real head, it would have a serious ache."

From the corner of my eye I could see the mother's lip curl into a slight smile. Odd, I thought, I didn't remember anything humorous on the patient information forms she was filling out. I pointed to the computer screen as discreetly as I could, then started typing. *Say something else.*

"Say something else?" asked Marmi. "Whatever do you mean?"

Something funny.

"Something funny? What do you think I am? Some desperate vaudevillian? A jokester? A merry widow?"

I typed again. *What's a merry widow?*

"Seriously. You couldn't derive the meaning from context, Sophie?"

The mother did what I thought she might if Marmaduke talked enough. She laughed.

We both gave her a look and she winked back. "You're a hoot," she whispered to Marmaduke.

Just then Dr. Callahan arrived on the scene, tall, confident, and doctorly. Moonflower was suspiciously absent. "So, is this Robert and Michael?" He peeked around the desk, smiling at the two boys who smiled back. He did have a way with kids. "Are their files ready?" he asked me.

The mother stood, handing me the clip board. "I'm sorry, I've been filling these out too slowly. The air here is a little..." she eyed him carefully before finishing her sentence. "Thick."

Dr. Callahan, somewhat befuddled by her comment, looked around the room as if he'd see the thick air himself and understand her better. "That's okay," he said finally, obviously still confused, "we can get started anyway. Sophie, will you bring me those files after you've entered the boys' information in the computer?"

"Will do, Dr. Callahan."

He gestured to the boys. "Robert, Michael, come along." They were up and moving, the mother following behind down the hall, but just before the exam room door closed, I heard her say, "Aha. There it is." I was very certain she wasn't talking about Dr. Callahan's exam equipment.

I entered the boys' information into the computer, put together two patient files, took them back to Dr. Callahan as he had requested, then set back to work organizing my project for promoting Dr. Callahan's practice. During the hour that he spent examining his two patients I managed to make a good amount of headway, in between phone calls and a drop-in salesman determined to peddle three pieces of artwork at cut-rate prices.

When I heard the exam room door open and Dr. Callahan's pleasant voice, I minimized my internet browser and opened the billing window, readying for my next orders. The boys tore around the corner of the desk and dropped to the floor again to play, while Dr. Callahan handed me to two files and gave the mother a forced smile.

"I'm looking forward to seeing you again," he said, shaking her hand. As Moonflower hovered around his right ear, he turned his head to me. "Sophie, Mrs. Wiley wants to make an appointment for Robert to return for more testing." He attempted a slight swat at Moonflower, hoping, I think, that Mrs. Wiley wouldn't notice. "That's a two hour appointment," he added, retreating back to his exam room.

Mrs. Wiley shook her head as if she felt sorry for the man, then gladly gave me her attention to make the appointment and pay for the eye exams. She was just putting her credit card away when, even from behind the closed door, we both heard the doctor chastising someone. I winced. When the lights flickered, Mrs. Wiley removed something else from her wallet and handed it to me. "Here." She placed a business card in my hand. "Give me a call if this gets too..." She waved her hand around for effect. "Wild." She threw me a wink then lowered her voice. "That spirit in there – she's on fire."

She rounded up her sons and headed out the door while I inspected the card. Nothing fancy – just plain white paper stock with black typeface. *Tara Wiley. Spiritual Medium. 555-3355.*

Aha! I was correct. She had seen Marmaduke. I tucked the card away safely in my purse hoping things would never get that wild, but thankful to have someone to call just in case.

CHAPTER NINE

The rest of the day proved touch and go for poor Dr. Callahan. Moonflower was stressing him terribly. I'd planned to tell him about the suspicious visitor and her co-hort, but decided it would add needlessly to his tense state. I'd already called the condo manager soon after it happened to let her know that we definitely had a situation on our hands. Beyond that, there was nothing to be done. Why make him more upset than he already was?

As we closed up for the night after the last patient, I decided to see if he knew anything about Jina Bhandari and her father.

"So," I started as casually as possible. "You just bought this office condo recently?"

He nodded while checking to make sure the coffee pot was off. "April."

"Was the previous owner nice?" I cringed inwardly at the silliness of the question. Luckily, he seemed distracted with checking lights around the office, and didn't seem to notice or care.

"Never met the owner," he said from down the hall. "The entire deal was handled through lawyers."

"The lawyers never said why the owner was selling?"

He returned to the waiting room, briefcase in hand, ghost companion close on his heels. He gave her an irritated glance, sighed, then answered my question. "Nope. I spent over an hour signing a mile-high stack of papers, and the place was mine. And now, so is the debt. Why?"

I grabbed my purse and positioned myself in front of the security alarm. "Ready?"

He placed his hand on the doorknob while I punched in the numbers. The unit beeped twice, Dr. Callahan opened the door and we exited, locking the door behind us. I smiled. "Yes! I got it right the first time." I raised my hand for a high five. The crooked smile curled on his lips and I swear, those blue eyes twinkled. When his hand slapped mine gently, I was aware of its warmth and for an instant, I imagined that hand caressing the small of my back. Nerves all over my body began to tingle from the short contact. My stomach knotted and my knees went wobbly.

And I don't think I was the only one affected by the touch. "So," he said, shoving the hand into his pants pocket, his cheeks pinking slightly. "I'm beginning to wonder if I did the right thing inviting the group to meet here. What do you think?"

I tried hard to push the hand-caressing-my-back thought from my head, but it wasn't easy. "What are you worried about?" I asked, throwing my purse over my shoulder in a move that was intended to appear cool and nonchalant. As if to say, *Yeah, I didn't just picture you stroking my naked body or wonder if your chest is as soft and smooth as your wonderfully warm hand.*

"Oh, I'm not really worried about anything, I guess. I'm just not ... really the hosting kind of guy, you know. And I don't want you to think I'm adding to your job duties or anything, because that's not what I meant to do. In fact, I don't want you to feel...you know...obligated."

"It's fine. They're a motley crew, but I think they'll grow on me. I'm looking forward to it."

"Yeah?"

"Yeah."

"And the job – is it growing on you too? Enough to stay?"

"Definitely. I really, really love...the job."

The hairs on my arms were standing on end. A result, I thought at first, of Dr. Callahan's endearing smile and my lingering lustful fantasy. But when Marmaduke appeared and whispered in my ear, I realized the culprit was Moonflower, who had drifted up to the branches of the dogwood, stewing up some electrical energy. One look at her wrathful eyes told me that I'd better say "goodnight, Doctor" and move out before another streetlight blew.

"See you tomorrow!" I waved and hoofed it to my car, leaving poor Cal...I mean, Dr. Callahan...in the dust looking a little bewildered.

At home I indulged in another dinner of salami, cheese, and crackers, chasing the delight with a penny-saving drink: a glass of tap water. It was a quiet and sort of lonely dinner. Marmaduke was absent, as he sometimes was. Unlike Moonflower, who seemed forever attached to poor Dr. Callahan, Marmaduke came and went without warning. Soon after we had met, I asked him about his habit of popping in and out. He admitted that even he didn't understand it entirely. He suspected his moments of "consciousness" as he called them, were connected to thought and energy in the physical plane. Oftentimes he was in control to come and go freely, yet there were times when he experienced a pull and then, the next thing he knew, there he was, in my world or out.

After stashing away the dwindling gift basket goodies, I slipped on my fuzzy gray cardigan and opened Peter Pan's cage. He was still slumbering peacefully in his hammock, but a little tap roused him. He poked his sweet, furry little head out, blinked twice, then scampered up my arm and onto my shoulder. I held a pecan treat up for him. He snatched it quickly with his two, tiny hands and began chewing greedily as if he might never eat again. His large, bulging eyes, which were perfectly designed for night vision, seemed to say, *Thank you, Sophie. I love you, but I think I love this pecan more.*

Once he consumed the nut, I removed him from my shoulder and placed him gently in the cardigan pocket. We were still a couple of hours from sunset – he'd likely rest in the pocket for a while before waking fully and tackling a night of rigorous exercise wheel workouts.

I plopped down on my couch. The worn springs creaked and sighed under my weight. Watching TV was out of the running for an evening activity since I'd canceled the cable. Food and gas were more important than mindless entertainment. Sadly, the one thing I really craved at the moment was mindless entertainment.

Uno must have sensed my disappointment because the cardboard box that served as his cat bed teetered as he pulled himself through the round cutout opening. He stretched, then made a leap for the couch, rubbing his pointy nose on my sweater, and purring in a sympathetic tone. At least I decided it was a sympathetic tone. He was probably communicating a desire to be fed.

I rubbed his neck with loving attention. "How are you tonight, Uno, old pal?"

He meowed in response, which I translated to, *Not so bad, Sophie, but how about you? You look sad.*

Another sigh escaped my throat. "Not sad really, just...frustrated I guess."

He meowed again. *You really like that Dr. Callahan, don't you?*

I stopped the neck rubbing and raised an eyebrow. "How do you know about Dr. Callahan?"

"Taken to fictional conversations with animals, have you?" asked Marmaduke as he appeared near the door, arms folded over his chest.

"How can I be sure that my conversations with you aren't fictional? For all I know, you could be a figment of my imagination. Maybe that psychiatrist was right. Maybe I'm a crazy narcissist."

He shook his head. "I'm very real. Just as real as your growing infatuation for Doctor Do Good."

"I thought you agreed he was a nice guy."

He sniffed. "True enough. He seems altruistic, self-sacrificing, magnanimous. A good egg."

"Then why the sarcasm?"

"Let's not waste our breath on my cynical tendencies, but instead focus on what you're going to do about this dark phantom that's getting in your way."

"I'm not infatuated, by the way."

"Oh, of course not. And I'm not incorporeal."

"No, I'm serious. Do I find him somewhat attractive? Sure. But I think a lot of guys are attractive. The checkout guy at the grocery store, for instance. He's cute. If you were alive, I'd think you were handsome. That doesn't mean I'm infatuated."

He cocked a brow at me. He thought I was full of it, and I probably was – but only mildly full of it. Infatuation was too strong a word. Enamored. I was sort of, maybe, possibly becoming a wee bit enamored.

"What I am," I continued, not copping to any sexual interest, "is concerned."

"Concerned?"

"That's right. For his business. If Moonflower keeps on like this, she's going to scare away all of his patients. And he's certainly never going to be able to keep a receptionist."

"And?"

"And what?"

"Well, then, what are you going to do about this...concern?"

I sat for a contemplative minute, having gone back to rubbing Uno's furry neck while he purred with pleasure. Of course, I knew exactly what he was getting at – that I should get on the phone with that mother who gave me her card.

"What if the lady tries to send you into the light like that last medium?" I asked him.

"It is very kind of you to be concerned, but do not trouble yourself with such mundane inanities – I can take care of myself. You take care of your...concern."

"Would you stop saying it like that?"

"Most sorry. Now, the card?"

Taking his cue, I went to my purse on the kitchen counter, retrieved the business card from the wallet, and dialed Tara Wiley, Spiritual Medium. She picked up on the third ring. "Thank goodness you called. I haven't been able to stop thinking about you since I left the office today."

Wow. She was talented. "Um...you know who this is?"

Her response was confident. "Sophie from Dr. Callahan's office?"

I was in awe. "That's so cool. I wish I could do that."

"You don't have caller ID on your phone?"

"Oh. Right. I see. You didn't pick up my...never mind."

"You don't know much about mediums, do you?"

"No."

"Well you should. You are one after all. But we can talk more about that later. It's nearly the witching hour around here, and by that, I mean that the boys are so revved up that I'll be getting on my broom soon. Let's get to the point: is that female spirit causing problems?"

"Is she ever."

"She's unique. Powerful. Hang on." She took a break to yell at her sons, but despite the fact that she'd obviously covered the phone with her hand, I could still hear her rebuke. "Robert! I told you to take that Lego out of your brother's ear or you'll be doing some serious contemplation time." Some muffled clattering and she was back with me. "I'm sorry about that. Where were we? Oh, yes. And she doesn't like you. Her...intense connection to Dr. Callahan feels almost frantic. Misdirected. There's something unnatural about her presence."

"You got all of that from seeing her just once?" I could hear Robert and Michael screaming in the background and felt guilty for keeping her on the phone.

"She's not your everyday run-of-the-mill ghost – that's for sure. Something kept nagging at me when I was driving home after our appointment, then it hit me while I was cooking the spaghetti. She's not residual."

A crash on the other end of the phone made me wince. "It sounds like I caught you at a bad time. Do you need to go?"

"Yes, but it's important you understand the anomaly here."

"What do you mean when you say she's not residual?"

"That's really my own term to describe what I believe is happening with this particular spirit. In the paranormal world, the term 'residual haunting' describes a lingering event that just keeps playing like a record that skips. For instance, a horrible car accident that ends fatally. Drivers on the road where that accident happened may report seeing a ghost image of that incident. That's a residual haunting. There is no interaction between the energy and the living. That isn't what I'm talking about here. What I mean when I say she's not residual is that her spirit didn't remain when her body died. She moved on. Again, this is just a suspicion based on my experience in Dr. Callahan's examination room."

"Why are we seeing her then? I mean, if you're right, and she did move on when she died."

"Someone would have summoned her to return."

Oh man. This was a little too creepy for my comfort. "Summoned? I don't like the sound of that."

"It's very possible that her presence is the product of witchcraft."

Marmi had been hovering over my shoulder during the unsettling phone conversation and didn't wait even a beat to plunge into interrogation when I clicked the receiver off. "What did she say?"

I rubbed my temples to ward off the headache that had appeared out of nowhere. "I must be losing my mind."

"She told you you're going mad? What kind of medium is this woman?"

Leaning against the counter for support, I attempted to keep the world from reeling around me. Witchcraft? That felt way too "out there" for my comfort. True, I talked to ghosts, so who was I to question. But witchcraft? To me, the idea was crazy and far-fetched. Kind of like alien visitations and Elvis sightings. In my mind, witches were only real on Halloween when people donned costumes and roamed the streets, and they certainly didn't have real powers or cast real spells.

Marmi wasn't appreciative of my quiet moment to contemplate. "Sophie, why does she think you're losing your mind?"

I blew out a releasing sigh. "She didn't tell me that I'm losing my mind. Do you believe in witches?"

"Is that what she said? Moonflower is a witch?"

"Marmi! Could you please just answer the question?"

"Yes."

"Yes, what? Yes, you believe in witches or yes you can answer the question?"

"You're making this very complicated."

"Marmi..."

"Yes, I can answer the question, and yes, I believe in witches. It was a witch that brought me here to America. My great aunt Nettie Jane. A trouble maker, she was."

"You're being serious. Your aunt was a witch?"

"Sadly, she couldn't cast a spell correctly to save her life. And her love potions..." He shook his head solemnly. "Let's just say she should have called them hate potions. It was my job to bring her home before she wreaked more havoc overseas."

"What happened?"

"She didn't put up a fight. She was quite pleased that her family cared enough to send me. Unfortunately, she cast a security spell on me to ensure our safe passage home, and minutes later I was dead in the middle of Main Street. Never saw that motor car coming."

I knew that Marmaduke's death had been the result of being struck by a car while crossing the street, but he had never mentioned the Great-Aunt-Nettie-Jane-the-witch connection. "I'm sure you loved your aunt, Marmi, but it seems a stretch to believe that the car ran you over because of a bad spell. I mean, accidents happen."

He shook his head again. "You don't understand. The vehicle had no driver."

"It slipped out of gear and rolled into you?"

He cast me a disapproving scowl. "The possessed jalopy ignited its own pistons and accelerated toward my exact location with the intent purpose of ending my life. Witnesses were frightened half out of their wits and Great Aunt Nettie Jane did retire from witching thereafter. I guess something good came of my demise, my termination, my exit to the afterlife." He paused, chewing on that last statement. After a few thought provoking moments, he stated matter-of-factly, "So, yes, dear Sophie. I believe in witches."

It was kind of hard to argue with Marmaduke after that story, if only because he was obviously sad recalling the event. And he was an awfully smart guy. If he believed a faulty witch's spell killed him, maybe he was right. I supposed I needed to consider that witches and witchcraft had to be as possible as ghosts who had a gift for gab.

"I'm sorry, Marmi," I said. "Sorry that the bewitched car killed you."

"Yes, well, it's all spilled milk now, as they say. I like to joke and say that Great Aunt Nettie Jane's security spell backfired on me." He chuckled at his own wit. "So, does this woman believe the good doctor's scary shadow is a witch?"

"No. She thinks witchcraft is responsible for calling her spirit back. You know – Moonflower died and moved on to wherever we go, then someone brought her back as a ghost."

"For what purpose?"

That's exactly what I wondered. If Jina was, in fact, Moonflower, who would want to raise her spirit and why? Was it her father? Maybe he missed her so much he resorted to magical means to see her again. Or maybe he regretted selling his office and was trying to scare Dr. Callahan away. Regardless, it seemed very likely that Jina Bhandari was the ghost calling herself Moonflower, and while I wasn't gutsy enough to call up her father and start asking questions, I did have access to someone who knew how she'd died.

"World to Sophie. Sophie, are you there?" Marmaduke's voice shook me from my trance.

"Sorry, Marm," I said, moving around the counter and grabbing my water glass for another drink. "I was thinking."

"You can disappear into your thoughts, can't you?"

Other thoughts were forming quickly in my mind, and I knew Marmi wouldn't approve, but I didn't care. I'd made a decision. I gulped the last of the water and set the glass down. "I'm going out."

CHAPTER TEN

Barney's Corner Pub was not the most popular drinking hole in Stephens City, but it had been my favorite for a very long time. True to its name, it sat on the corner of Main Street and Washington Way. The dark, but welcoming bar held both good memories and bad. Good, because that's where I met Marmaduke. Bad, because that's where I broke up with Shane. And I hadn't been back since, because it was also his favorite hangout.

My choice to drop in for a beer and cheesy fries wasn't driven by thirst, although a cold beer did sound especially tantalizing. And it certainly wasn't driven by any sudden affluence. I shouldn't be spending the money, but the fact of the matter was, I had at least a ninety-percent chance of running into Shane since cops and firefighters drank for half-price on Thursdays, and he had a habit of partaking in the benefit weekly.

I had no romantic motivation for meeting up with Shane, but he was the responding policeman the day Jina Bhandari died, so it was very likely, with the right amount of eyelash batting, that I could wheedle a decent amount of information out of him on the subject. True, I could have just called him, but I didn't want to give him any ideas or stroke his enormous ego. No, this way I could feign a craving for cheesy fries and a forgetfulness that it was Thursday night. He wasn't quite bright enough to see through my ruse, I was pretty sure.

Marmaduke, however, clued in the minute I pulled on the heavy oak door. He had vanished when I announced that I would be going out, and reappeared just as I was walking into the warm, loud bar. "I suppose that you are unlikely to heed any advice I might offer, but I shall make my voice heard regardless – this is a mistake of grand proportions."

"That sounds like a statement, not advice, Marmi. Besides, I'm just getting a beer and some fries," I whispered under my breath while sitting my rump on a barstool right in front of the establishment's namesake. "Hiya, Barney! Long time, no see."

Barney was the biggest, sweetest teddy bear of a man that ever existed. He literally looked like a teddy bear. Big tummy, chubby cheeks, furry face, relentless smile. He was super huggable. "Sophie!" The smile grew extra-wide as he towel-dried a hefty mug. "I knew you'd come back one day. The place hasn't been the same without you." He held up the dry mug. "The usual?"

Marmaduke grumbled in my ear. "You haven't been here since you bid farewell to that rounder, Shane."

My plan required the appearance of sanity, so answering Marmi's complaints was out of the question. He'd have to be ignored. "Um..." I squirmed on my stool. "Things are a little tight for me right now, Barney, what do you have on draft that's a little less expensive than my usual?" I coughed. "Actually, what's the cheapest thing you have?"

He gave me an understanding nod, positioned the mug under a spigot and pulled, allowing the amber ale to flow. "That's Pabst. And don't worry. This first one is on me. Cheesy fries?"

"Yes, please." I couldn't hide my excitement. Barney served the best cheesy fries in North America. Possibly the world. "Just a half-order though." I wagged a finger at him. "And no charity. I'll pay. I may be poor, but I'm not destitute." I sipped off a bit of the head from the mug he'd set in front of me. "I'm finally employed again. Get my first paycheck tomorrow."

"Congratulations!" Barney's eyes twinkled. When his hair turned gray, he'd definitely look like Santa Claus. "I'll get that order in." He disappeared into the kitchen.

I swept an inconspicuous glance around the bar. No Shane.

Marmaduke jumped on the moment. "See. He isn't here. Let us withdraw while you have a chance to escape disaster."

I lifted the mug to my lips readying for a sip, but whispered discreetly first. "I'm waiting for my cheesy fries."

He huffed. "This has nothing to do with food or drink."

I shrugged and turned my stool to peruse the bar's patrons more thoroughly. I spotted Jenn Evans cuddling up to Alex Turner, but those were the only familiar faces. Apparently, some things never changed. Jenn was a dispatcher at Stephens City PD and Alex was an officer just barely out of the academy. Jenn had been crushing on him from the first day he went on duty, but he seemed only to enjoy the attention. Jenn noticed me watching them and winked. I raised my glass, then turned around just in time to be greeted by my steamy half-order of cheesy fries. I rubbed my hands together before digging in. "Barney, you don't know how I've missed these!"

Marmaduke paced behind me, his hands clutched together behind his back. "Fish and chips from McDougals. Now there's a dish worthy of such accolade. Extolment. Applause. Those 'fries,' as you call them, appear to have been drowned in a yellow ooze not fit for consumption. But please, do inhale them so we may vacate this saloon post haste and abandon your barmy scheme."

Barmy. That was a new one. Probably meant crazy or crack-pot based on the context, but truthfully, I didn't care. Yes, I had come in hopes of bumping into Shane, but the delectable and very fattening junk food had taken center stage, and Marmaduke's fears be damned, I was going to enjoy every heart-clogging bite.

The problem with cheesy fries, however, is the very thing that makes them so holy: the cheese. It has this slimy tendency to drip from the fry as it's entering the mouth, landing on the lower lip and sliding down the chin. The bigger the drip, the drippier a person looks when someone walks into the bar where those fries are being devoured. In my case, the gloppy drip of cheese was colossal, and I failed to wipe it away before the big oak door opened and Shane entered. I froze. How does one appear graceful when one's face is smeared with gelatinous goop?

Marmaduke was beside himself with anxiety over my ex's arrival. He paced and chattered endlessly. Luckily, I was the only one who could hear his raving.

It took Shane all of one-millionth of a second to spot me. A grin tugged slowly at the corners of his perfect lips and he sauntered my way. "Hey, Soph." He leaned on the bar.

Were I to respond instantly, potato and cheese would have spewed all over the clean t-shirt that clung so finely to his well-chiseled chest beneath. That would have served him right for the way he'd treated me in the past, but I didn't need the embarrassment, so I chewed, swallowed, wiped my chin, chased it all with a swig of beer, then returned the greeting. "Hey, Shane." I performed an exaggerated peek behind him. "All alone tonight? No Amy Amy Bo Bamey?"

He rolled his eyes but sat next to me despite the jab. "She's working."

I nodded, feeling the tiniest bit guilty for hating Amy as much as I did. She was a nurse, after all. Worked the ER. She saved lives for crying out loud. She was actually a nice person and we'd been pretty good friends before Shane dumped me for her. If I wanted to be entirely honest with myself, Shane was a rebound hook-up, and probably destined for failure anyway. The breakup before Shane was far more devastating – the man far more painful to forget. That had been, in my mind, a true love, with only one obstacle – the man's wife. Yeah, I thought, I really should grow up and forgive Shane and Amy.

Shane raised his hand to signal Barney. "Give me a Dos Equis, would ya man?"

"In a sec, Shane."

"And two shots of Beam," Shane added, knocking my elbow with his. "Like the old days."

I shook my head and held up a fending hand. "No, no. Not for me. Can't hold my whiskey anymore, and I certainly can't afford it."

"It's on me. Come on."

"Oh, Lord..." I heard Marmi moan.

"I don't know..."

"Just one. Then I promise I won't bug you anymore."

Well, I did need to stick around. I'd come with a purpose and that purpose was to talk to Shane. Agreeing to join Shane in a drink would set the friendly tone I needed for opening up the Jina Bhandari discussion. What could one shot hurt? Nothing, I justified. The problem with justifications: they always bite me in the butt. "Okay," I agreed. "Just one."

"It begins," moaned Marmi some more.

Barney set the shot glasses down and filled them to the brim. He shot me a wink. "Two of my favorite people drinking together again."

I lifted the shot ready to pound it. "Don't get used to it, Barney. It's just for old times' sake." Having made my position clear, I threw back the glass and let the warm, biting liquid slide down my throat. My eyes watered as I snapped the glass back to the counter with a *clack!* Nice. Immediately, my body relaxed. I chased the Jim Beam with the rest of my cheap beer and turned to give Shane a once over. The whiskey must have affected my vision, because suddenly he looked ten times more appealing than when he walked in. The bulging muscles of his biceps bulged more, his dark, wavy hair waved more, and his intensely dark eyes...I leaned closer to him, resting a hand on the back of his barstool. "You are one hunk of handsome, aren't you?"

Marmaduke had apparently had enough. "That's it!" he shouted. And disappeared.

I marched forward, my justifications fueling my ridiculous behavior. Had to butter Shane up. Learn more about Jina Bhandari.

Shane, following my lead, leaned in as well, a devilish grin erupting across his sexy-stubbled face. "I like you in short hair. Very Halle Berry."

Now, the thing is, Shane was practically Greek-god-gorgeous head to toe, yet, I suddenly realized that was something was missing. The urge to wrap myself around his rock-hard abs and practically melt into him. Desire. Lust. Nervous butterflies. They were all gone. I had finally reached the point where I could take him or leave him. I pulled back and teased, "Well, you have a girlfriend, sir, so this..." I fanned my hand across my body like Vanna White presenting a new board of letters. "This is off limits. No touchy, touchy."

"Understood," he agreed, settling back onto his stool. He was still awfully cocky-confident for himself. "How about we celebrate the forging of a new friendship with another shot of whiskey?"

I gave it a moment's thought. "Sure," I said. "But one condition."

"What would that be?"

"Tell me a little about Jina Bhandari."

Shane waved his hand in the air. "Two more shots, Barn!" He turned his attention back to me. "I swear, I didn't sleep with anyone named Jina."

"No, you dope. Jina Bhandari. The girl who died in Dr. Callahan's office last year. Before it was his office. You were the responding officer."

It took him a second, but recognition eventually lit on his face. "The college girl," he said with a nod. "Why do you want to know about her?"

Hmm. That was a good question. I should have anticipated it and planned how to answer that one in advance. Too late for shoulda-woulda-couldas. I shrugged. "When you hear that someone died in the same place where you work, you get a little curious." My response wasn't the smartest lie in the world, but it passed muster for Shane's limited wit, evidently.

"What do you want to know?" he asked, throwing back the second shot.

"How did she die?"

He flicked a glance at my full shot glass. "Drink up and I answer."

Just like Shane. I obeyed, and my eyes watered again. My body started to weaken all over like just-cooked spaghetti.

Shane laughed. "One thing you have over Amy – you know how to drink some whiskey."

I glowered inside at his backhanded compliment, which implied that Amy had an awful lot over me. I scowled inwardly, but smiled outwardly to keep the momentum going. "Gee, thanks. Back to the college girl."

"She was pregnant."

"She died giving birth in the office?"

"No. You're really cute when you're drunk."

"I'm not drunk."

"That's debatable. I arrived after the EMTs who had tried, unsuccessfully, to revive her. The father claimed that they had been having an argument and she just collapsed in front of him. Given his claim and the claims of witnesses who over-heard the argument, foul play was considered, but the coroner's report showed she died of some sort of...hemorrhage." He shook his head, seeming to rethink what he'd said. "No, hemorrhage wasn't the word." His index finger tapped the bar while his brain churned. "What's that called when there's a clot – a blood clot?"

"Aneurism?"

He snapped his fingers. "That's it. She died of a rare pregnancy-related aneurism."

"Was the father horribly upset?"

"One more whiskey and I'll answer that for you."

"Jeez, you're a cad."

He laughed. "A cad? Sounds like you've been talking to that ghost from Ireland again."

England you dip wad. I raised my hand and hollered, "Two more shots, Barney ol' pal!"

Barney was filling two beer orders for a couple at the end of the bar. He raised an eyebrow at me. "You sure, Soph?"

"Sure, I'm sure," I slurred. One more. I could handle it. The room started to spin a little. I was Sophie, the whiskey drinking, short-haired, ex-girlfriend, after all. "Put it right here!" I slapped the counter top in front of me. I should have realized I was already heavily anesthetized when no pain reg-istered from the impact, the resulting sound of which caused half the bar to turn my way. But then again, that's the prob-lem with whiskey. Two shots in, you think you can drink the whole bottle and still calculate complex algebraic equations in your head. I slammed that third sucker down, then stood and moved in close to Shane's face. "Tell me: did the father sheem horribbily upshet?"

"Why do you care?"

The floor started to sway underneath my feet. Maybe three shots was too much...

"Why don't you care?" I retorted. Even in my drunken state (Shane was right about that), I detected that the question was strange and non-sequitur. It got me what I was looking for though.

"I did care, actually," he said. "Because he didn't seem that upset. His reaction was odd. That's why I was suspicious. But like I said, it all checked out, so who knows why people react the way they do, right? Whoa. Sophie – you'd better sit back down."

Shane's face had gone blurry and my stomach was starting to churn. I made an attempt at aiming my buttocks for the stool, but missed, and fell on the floor. "Uh-oh!" I laughed. "That stool moved!" I laughed some more and raised an arm which Shane grabbed to hoist me back up.

"I think I'd better drive you home," he said.

"That's okay," a voice said from out of nowhere. Actually, it wasn't out of nowhere, but with the room spinning, it felt like that to me. While I had fallen to the floor, Dr. Callahan had entered the bar. He stood between Shane and me, then slipped a firm arm around my waist. "Cal!" I bellowed, grin-ning from ear to ear. "How are you?"

He smiled. "I'm fine. You doing okay?"

"Been soberererer..."

He turned to Shane. "From what she tells me, you're not the greatest influence on her. I'll drive her home. She's the only receptionist I have."

"You smell good," I said. "Did I ever tell you how good you smell?"

Shane raised his hands defensively. "Hey, man. She's a grown woman. I didn't force her to do those shots."

Cal raised his eyebrows to express skepticism, but didn't respond. He caught Barney's attention. "How much is her bill?"

"Hey," Shane interrupted. "I've got it. You okay going home with this guy, Soph?"

I nodded. "He's Cal. Doctor Cal Callahan. He's my bosh. He's a cool bosh. And cute too, don'tchoo think?" My foot gave way under me, but Cal held me tight.

"Let's go," he said.

When we were near the door, I tried like heck to focus clearly on his magnificent face and to speak without slurring any words. "I said Shane was a bad influence? I don't remember that." I think I managed not to slur, but focusing was harder.

"No," he smiled. "Marmaduke told me. How do you think I knew where you were?"

Good ol' Marmi. He was such a good ghost-friend. The best a girl could have.

CHAPTER ELEVEN

I woke up the next morning, my tongue practically super-glued to the top of my mouth, and Marmaduke staring me in the face. "Get up. He's going to be here soon."

While invisible hammers pounded on my temples, I tried to process his meaning. Who? Who was going to be where soon? My hand fumbled around the side table for my cell phone. The alarm function was functioning perfectly. And way too loudly. I squinted my eyes to force a focus of my vision, but my fingers weren't cooperating well enough to tap the proper shut-off button. Three random swats at the screen did the trick though. I squinted again to see the time. Eight forty-five a.m. That seemed awfully late. My mouth was so dry, it actually hurt to talk. "How long has this been ringing?" I asked Marmi.

"Too long. You agreed to be ready by nine."

I fell back on my pillow. "Ready for what?"

"Work. The good doctor is picking you up, and then driving you to your car, which you left at the bar last night."

Those last words brought the entire previous night back to me in hideous detail. From the delicious fries, to Shane and the three shots, and then my blush-inducing flirtation with Dr. Callahan. If memory served right, I talked about how good he smelled, how cute he was, and how sweet and kind he was. Over and over and over again. Even as he was closing the door and telling me he'd be back this morning at nine. I sat up straight, both terrified and mortified. I had fifteen minutes to get ready. I stumbled to the bathroom, pulled back the shower curtain and turned both the cold and hot water knobs to start the water flowing.

While it warmed, I took two aspirin and gulped them down with cold water straight from the sink. My shower was a three-minute quickie. Just enough to get the job done. I think I even forgot to condition. My stomach was too sour for breakfast, but not sure if I'd be hungry for lunch, I fumbled around the kitchen in my robe fixing a sandwich, just in case.

"Was it terrible, Marmi?" I asked him while haphazardly knifing egg salad onto a slice of wheat toast.

"To what are you referring? Your drunkedness?"

"No. I know that was bad. My throbbing head is reminding me very well, thank you. I mean, the flirting. With Dr. Callahan. Did I totally embarrass myself?"

"You did not seem embarrassed last night."

"Should I be embarrassed today?"

"You referred to him fifteen times as your 'Cal Pal.'"

"You're exaggerating."

"I counted. And you sniffed him a lot."

"Yeah. It's that cologne. He smells so good."

"Oh, he knows that now."

I slipped the sandwich into a plastic baggie then stumbled back to my bedroom, taking all of one minute to slip into a navy pair of capri pants, a floral sleeveless number that matched enough to get by, and a beige pair of flats that I usually only wore with jeans because they were so old and worn, but quite frankly, they'd just have to suffice for the day.

I took a quick swipe through my hair with a comb and thanked my lucky stars that I'd cut it so short – the style didn't require much care. A little blush and mascara and I had to call myself made-up, because just then, the doorbell rang. Of course. Of course he was on time. He was just that kind of guy. The kind of guy who set a date and kept it to the second. So sweet, and yet, at that very moment, I could have done with a little tardiness.

At the door, I froze with my hand on the knob, my palms sweaty with dread. The thought of opening the door and having to face my actions from the night before was so intense that my heart raced. I could feign alcohol-induced amnesia. That would get us both off the hook. He had to be as embarrassed as I was. More even. He was a boss with this employee that couldn't hold her liquor or her libido. Maybe he'd fire me. Geez. Just when I found a job with promise.

"You must turn the knob to actually open the door, Sophie," Marmaduke urged.

The doorbell rang again, startling me into swinging the door open, and declared with way too much enthusiasm, "You're here! Come in! I'm almost ready."

He stepped in with what I detected as a hint of reluctance. Meanwhile, I babbled like a lunatic and ran around the apartment grabbing up various items I needed for the day. Keys. I needed my car keys. They were probably in my purse, but I had better check. "So, hey, thanks so much for this. And for last night. That was really, really nice of you. And way, way above and beyond your duties as my boss." Keys not in purse. Darn. Where were they? "You know, I just went there for the cheesy fries. Those shots of whiskey...well...sorry, I'm looking for my car keys. I might have left them in my bedroom. I'll be right back." I needed my cell phone anyway. Probably the keys were on my bed stand next to the phone. Kill two birds with one stone and all of that. "So I hope you didn't have to travel too far...I mean, I don't know where you live, but I hope it's not too far from..." Keys not on the night stand. I grabbed up my phone then trudged back to the living room, placed my hands on my hips and frowned deeply. "My keys weren't in there either. I guess this is one of those moments when I have to back track and..." Suddenly it occurred to me that finishing my thought would lead directly into territory I had hoped to avoid conversationally. "Keys. Can't live with 'em, can't live without 'em, huh?" I said instead.

"You're very talkative in the morning, aren't you?" Dr. Callahan finally broke his own silence. At least he was smiling.

"Huh! Yeah, well, not usually." Don't ask me why, but at that very moment, I remembered the previous evening. Dr. Callahan was inching the door closed in a frantic attempt to escape my overbearing eagerness to fawn over him. I said a final goodbye as the door clicked shut, flipped the lock on the knob, stumbled to Peter Pan's cage and took him out for a quick kiss and cuddle. I had dropped my keys on the floor in front of the cage to free my hands. "Of course!" I slapped my forehead. "Peter Pan's cage..." I spun around to find my keys lying right where they'd fallen the night before.

Meanwhile, Dr. Callahan must have been perusing my apartment. "Oh, you like almonds too," he said.

I heard the words, but didn't really register their importance until, when picking my keys up from the floor, I noticed that the cage door was open. Not good. Why was Peter Pan's cage door open and not closed?

"You really should keep the lid on. Almonds can go stale like anything else." From the periphery of my sight and awareness, I saw him moving toward the almond can on my kitchen counter.

"Umm..." I was too slow. Disaster was most certain. Dr. Callahan had reached the can and picked it up to slip the lid on.

His eyes nearly popped out of his head. "Furry mouse!" he shouted. "Furry mouse!" The can flew high into the air, propelled by Dr. Callahan's startled toss, and when it landed on the floor, Peter Pan scampered, screeching his little flying squirrel screech. He turned in circles first, then, gaining his bearing, tore for cover under the couch. Poor little guy. I had fallen asleep with him cuddling me, so he never made it back to his cage. He must have crawled into the almond can after a night of frolicking around the apartment like a teenager whose parents were away for the weekend. I cringed, wondering what kind of damage he'd done.

"That mouse has a very furry tail!" Dr. Callahan shouted. "You should call an exterminator."

"That's Peter Pan, and he's not a mouse. He's a flying squirrel."

"You have a flying squirrel?" His hand was still on his chest.

"Long story." I pushed him toward the door. "He's a little scared now. You, um...wait out in the hall..." I opened the door and shoved him out. "I'll handle this and be right out." I winced. "Sorry. Just one minute."

Peter Pan was pretty terrorized, but he allowed me to scoop him up once I moved the couch and talked to him very sweetly.

"Great," I told Marmaduke, as I collected my purse, phone, lunch, and keys. "If he didn't think I was a total zero before, I'm sure he does now. He'll probably give me my notice when he drops me off at my car. Pink slip, here I come."

"I hardly think you have cause to worry. Did you hear the shrill pitch of his cry? He's probably far more concerned, and rightly so, that you are questioning his masculinity."

The drive to my car was a quick five minute jaunt, but felt like twenty grueling hours of strained conversation. Well, I guess conversation isn't exactly the right word. More like twenty hours of strained babbling. From me. Dr. Callahan was oddly quiet and distracted. I imagined he was mentally rehearsing the best way to give me the boot. Would he do it when he dropped me off at my car or wait until I arrived at the office? That would be cruel if he waited. A rip-it-off-like-a-band-aid approach at my car would be the most humane. Possibly I should make it easier for him and offer to leave? And would it be too much to ask for my pay for the three days I'd worked? These worrisome thoughts bounced off the walls of my brain endlessly while I blathered on how I'd come to parent a flying squirrel and a one-eyed cat.

Truthfully, I've found both stories to be an ice breaker, so I knew something was wrong when he barely nodded during my monologue. And I really knew something was wrong when my description of how Uno lost his eye didn't produce the slightest cringe. Everyone cringes at that story – even a Navy Seal who'd seen some grisly action in Afghanistan winced. It's most definitely cringe-worthy, and yet, all I got from Dr. Callahan was a "huh."

As we pulled next to my Honda in the now-empty parking lot of Barney's, Dr. Callahan finally spoke. "See you at the office." Short, but sweet. At least he didn't say, *See you...never again. You're fired, sucka.*

I decided to be brave and ask a tough question. "Are you upset with me?"

The question seemed to shake him out of some sort of trance. He turned in his seat and gave me a serious, thoughtful look. "Upset with you? Why would I be upset with you?"

"For getting drunk last night. Making you come pick me up, and then again today." I didn't mention the flirting. That was too embarrassing to confront. "I mean, I'd understand if you were. Who wants their employee causing them problems? Right?"

"No, no, no. You're not causing me problems. You're solving my problems."

"I am?"

"You're the best receptionist I've ever had. Don't get me wrong, I'd be happy if you'd stay away from that Shane guy. I don't care if he's a cop or not, he's obviously not good for you, but that's just my personal...opinion. And it has nothing to do with your job."

"Okay. It was just...you were so quiet this morning. You know. And last night..."

"I just have things on my mind. Nothing to do with you." He intensified his tone, emphasizing his point. "At all."

"Okay."

"Which reminds me, I'll be leaving early today. I have an appointment at one o'clock. You may have seen it blocked out in the appointment book."

"Yeah. I did, when I was confirming patients yesterday. Everything okay?"

He shrugged. "Eh."

An awkward silence ensued, which he eventually ended by pointing to the clock on his dash. "We'd better get going."

I nodded, collected my purse, and opened the door. "Right. See you at the office in a few then."

The furrows in his forehead vanished and a hint of that crooked smile returned. "Yup."

I wish I could say that things got better at work, but it just wasn't going to be that kind of Friday. Apparently, Moonflower had abandoned her job as Dr. Callahan's shadow to spend some quality time destroying the office.

I walked in to witness what appeared to be the aftermath of a tornado. My first thought was that the mystery boy and girl had broken in and robbed him. I felt immediately guilty that I hadn't warned him sooner. But it didn't take me long to determine who the true perpetrator was since she was still hard at work.

Moonflower was behind the reception desk lifting items one at a time, flinging them through the air to land wherever their trajectory led. The floor was strewn with overturned chairs, papers, file folders, pens and pencils, a mug, the computer mouse, a phone receiver, and Post-it Notes.

Dr. Callahan must have arrived just seconds before me because he stood, stupefied, still holding his briefcase.

Moonflower had just raised a stapler into the air when Dr. Callahan dropped the briefcase and raised his hands motioning her to stop.

"Moonflower," he pleaded. "Please. I'm begging you."

The stapler dangled mid-air while she registered his plea. "Johnny," she cooed. "I don't want you to beg."

"Then why are you doing this to me? Can't you see this is how I make my living?"

The stapler dropped like a rock onto the desk, and the clank made me flinch. Moonflower's eyes softened as she floated to him. "I'm sorry. Sometimes...things come over me. I don't know what happens to me."

Leaning over to pick up a file at my feet, I said nonchalantly, "It's okay, Jina, I'll clean this up."

Moonflower didn't respond in any way. Not even the little flicker like the time I tried using the name Jina on her the previous day. She never took her eyes off of Dr. Callahan.

His ears, however, perked up. "Who's Jina?"

I shook the file folder around and acted as if I'd just made a silly mistake. "I meant to say Moonflower. She just...reminds me of a girl I used to know named Jina." I emphasized the name Jina, but it still didn't elicit any sort of recognition from the calamitous ghost. Boy, she was a piece of work.

Marmaduke appeared next to me and whispered in my ear. "My, my, but she does have a violent streak, doesn't she?"

I rolled my eyes. She had a streak alright. A freaky streak. We had ten minutes before the first patient arrived, so I needed to get some tidying done post-haste. "Dr. Callahan, do you want to take her back with you so I can get this place presentable again?"

"Good idea." He threw me a look of apology and hastened Moonflower to follow him to his exam room.

"She didn't seem to recognize the name Jina when I threw it out there," I said while getting on my hands and knees to collect the debris left in the wake of her tantrum. The paper clips alone were strewn from one wall to the other. I sighed. "Maybe we're completely off base."

"An idea comes to mind."

I dumped paper clips in a pile on the front desk, and started setting the chairs upright. "What's your idea?"

"The realtor fellow. He knows what the young girl looked like."

I gave the waiting room a final once-over to make sure I hadn't missed a stray pen or paper clip, then set to work tidying my work space. Thank goodness she didn't mess with the computer. "He hasn't admitted that he sees ghosts. How can we ask him to identify her?"

"I wasn't suggesting we be so bold or forward as to invite him for that purpose. That would be most awkward. However, were he to be here at the same time she was moping around... possibly one thing would lead to another..."

"You're pretty crafty for a dead guy."

"Yes, well, I aim to please, as you Americans say."

"I don't know. Maybe we could give it a try. Or maybe she'll calm down soon and she'll cease to be a problem."

"No."

"What do you mean, no?"

"Drats. I was attempting a contemporary sarcastic retort and failed. Let me give it another go. Say it again."

"Say what again?"

"That wild fantasy about the violent ghost calming down. Repeat it for me."

I rolled my eyes. "Um... or maybe she'll calm down and won't be a problem anymore."

Marmaduke snorted. "Not." He maintained a deadpan expression for several seconds, then puffed up, very proud of himself. "There. Did I perform the modern-day jibe correctly?"

"Yes, wise guy, you performed correctly." I clipped the receiver back into the telephone unit and smiled. "I need to listen to messages. We'll talk about your idea later."

He made an imaginary gun from his thumb and index finger, aiming it in my direction. "Gotcha."

Marmaduke, when attempting to be more American, was funnier than a night at the local comedy club.

Dr. Callahan's morning was light as far as patients went, but that didn't stop Moonflower from doing her best to terrorize the few people who had appointments. His ten o'clock was a kindergartener named Caroline. While her mother filled out forms in the waiting room, Moonflower knocked a framed print off the far wall, causing glass to shatter. The incident also visibly rattled both mother and daughter's nerves, but luckily no one was hurt.

While Dr. Callahan examined little Caroline, I picked up shards of glass, hoping that would be the extent of our troubled ghost's hauntings – at least for the rest of their exam time.

I thought we were scot-free until Caroline's mother stood before me, trying to decide on a follow-up appointment time that would work for her schedule. She tapped her pen on the counter, staring at the small pocket calendar in front of her. "Fridays are always best I guess. But it would have to be in the morning, like today. Caroline has afternoon kindergarten. How about..."

I cringed as her inquiry was interrupted by Moonflower's cacophonous banshee wail with a bass tone so intense, it actually shook the walls.

Mother and daughter screamed simultaneously, while the wail continued on like a broken smoke detector that won't stop even when bashed to smithereens.

"What is that awful noise?" shouted the mother, covering her ears.

"Mommy, I'm scared!" yelled Caroline.

"Our neighbors, I think," I lied. "They must have a stereo." Just then, I spotted Dr. Callahan in the hallway, looking determined to save the day, but not knowing how. "It must be those neighbors again, don't you think, Dr. Callahan? With the loud stereo?" I turned back to the mother. "I'll ask them to turn it down when we're done here."

"Oh, we're done here!" shouted the mother while Caroline's pleas grew in urgency. She packed her checkbook and pocket calendar into her purse and turned to leave with her petrified child. I don't think she was buying my stereo ruse.

"Would you like me to call you to schedule that follow-up?" I shouted after her.

"No thank you! I'll call you..." And the door slammed behind them. When the door slammed, the wailing ended as quickly as it had started and the walls stopped rattling.

The chick had some awesome powers, I had to give her that. She could move objects and make sounds the living could hear two counties over.

"Did we lose them?" he asked when the mayhem ended.

"I think so." I slumped in my chair and banged my ear trying to stop the ringing. "Can't you stop her like you did earlier?"

"I don't even see her anymore, do you?"

"No."

"Oh, she's here," offered Marmaduke. "I can feel her, but she's...it's the oddest thing, but I'm without words to describe the sensation."

"Now he's without words," grumbled Dr. Callahan, running his hands through his hair. "What's going on here? I can't afford much more of this." He stormed back into his exam room and slammed the door shut.

I winced at the slamming and then wondered if I should remind him of his twelve-o'clock appointment. Best to let him cool down a few. If we could make it through one more appointment, he'd be off to his other business and hopefully things would settle.

"Marmi?" I asked. "Do you still feel her around?"

"Very definitely. You do not?"

"Actually, I do. I just didn't know how to explain it."

"Precisely. I know the man is under a good deal of stress, but his comment cut me to the quick, I will say."

The problem with having a friend whose 'body' is of the spirit realm, is the fact you can't touch them, hug them, or place a consoling pat on their shoulder. I gave him a look to let him know I was sorry, then continued on with my thoughts. "Before, I felt her presence when she let me see her, but now...I can't see her, but I feel like she's..." I imagined a room that filled with gas – the more gas that went into the room, the more you could smell it, but still could never see it. "It's like she's grown."

"Yes. The fiend is larger in spirit now. More powerful."

I placed my head in my hands. "Oh boy. Why couldn't I find a normal ghost-free job?"

CHAPTER TWELVE

D r. Callahan's twelve o'clock patient was a Mr. Yeltsin who only came in for yearly exams. Apparently, the elderly man had completed a vision therapy program several months earlier to eliminate double vision, and now saw Dr. Callahan for routine follow-ups. Surprisingly, Moonflower didn't throw anything, knock anything over or down, and didn't emit so much as a whimper.

Marmaduke came to the same conclusion I'd been chewing on. "She's only bothered by females," he said as Mr. Yeltsin left the office.

Dr. Callahan had been standing behind me. "That's what I was thinking," he said, three deep creases forming on his frowning forehead. "And that has to stop. I can't limit myself to male patients. I'll never make a living. Not to mention it's probably sexism and I'd lose my license." He lifted his briefcase onto my reception desk and tossed some files in, then clamped it shut. "Well, if you see her again, feel free to tell her that she's ruining my life." He pulled the briefcase from the desk and turned to leave. "I'm gone for the day. Sophie, feel free to leave as well. No reason for you to stay."

"I'll stay, if you don't mind. I need the work."

"I'll pay you for the full day."

"Right. About that – you said you could pay me today..."

He slapped his head. "Right. Sorry." He reached into his shirt pocket and pulled out a folded envelope. "Here. Your first week's pay. Really. Go."

I took the envelope gladly, and smiled, so thankful to have some money. "Nope. I have plenty to get done."

He tipped his head, giving up. "Okay then. Well, I'll see you Monday."

"Have a good weekend!" I waved. I was trying to cheer him up since his slumping shoulders told me he was way down in the dumps.

He waved back and let the door close behind him.

"That," said Marmi, "is not a happy man."

"I know," I agreed. "It makes me sad." I snatched the letter opener from a cup of pens on the desk, ran a clean slit through, and pulled out the check. Well, it wasn't a windfall, but it would keep me eating, put a little gas in the car and help toward an impending rent payment. I kissed the sweet prize and decided that it would be best to get it to the bank before the two o'clock cut-off for deposits. Otherwise I wouldn't have access to the money until Tuesday. I pulled my purse out of the corner and dug around for my car keys and sunglasses. "I'm going to the bank," I said to Marmi. "You coming?"

"I think I will stay put and see if the gloomy diva shows herself."

"Don't eat my egg salad sandwich," I teased him.

"Righto. I shall resist the urge."

I'd hoped to only be out ten minutes or so, but the Friday traffic was worse than I'd anticipated. Luckily, my bank has a drive-thru ATM, so that part of my errand was easy peasy, in and out. Then I decided to treat myself to fries and a Coke at McDonald's. Given the lunch hour, that took way longer than it should have.

By the time I pulled back into the parking lot, I'd been gone nearly forty-five minutes and had become drenched in sweat from the persistent heat and humidity. I was desperate for air conditioning. As I approached the office, I spotted Ronald Ellison peeking through the glass door. That, in and of itself, wasn't so odd. What did take me by surprise was the fact that Marmaduke stood next to him, chatting him up. And Mr. Ellison was answering.

"Hello..." I ventured hesitantly, not exactly sure of what had transpired during my absence, although I had my suspicions.

Startled, Ronald spun around. "I'm so sorry!" he yelped.

I threw Marmi a what-are-you-up-to glance while addressing Ronald's strange apology. "Sorry about what?"

He began to sputter out incomplete thoughts. "I was just... it's just that...he...this is all new..."

"We've talked," interrupted Marmaduke. "He knows everything."

"Can we finish this inside?" begged Ronald, glancing fearfully around. "I don't want Dory to know about this. She's not a believer."

"Sure." I slipped my key into the lock and a second later the two of us were sighing from relief. Me, because of the cool air, Mr. Ellison, I surmised, because he felt safe from being caught as a weirdo who thinks he sees ghosts. Nearly tap dancing from what I assumed were nerves, he made another request. "Could you, um, just lock the door while we talk? This is all so..." he waved his hands in the air and made a whistling noise. "It's all so out there. I can't have anyone labeling me as insane or anything, you know?"

I nodded understandingly. "Absolutely."

He whispered. "We're alone, right? I mean, besides Mr. Duke."

Marmi rolled his eyes. "Not Mr. Duke. Marmaduke. Marmaduke Dodsworth of Dartford in Kent."

"Yes," I assured him, "we're alone. Well, except maybe for another ghost."

His eyes widened and his head wobbled like a bobble head. "Jina?"

"We think so. We were hoping you could tell us, only she's not showing herself today."

He pulled his head into his shoulders like a turtle taking cover, and scanned the office with a set of fearful eyes. Poor Mr. Ellison was obviously traumatized by his gift. So much so that it was almost comical to watch. "Mr. Ellison..."

"Call me Ron." His eyes kept darting around the room in a paranoid fashion.

"Um, Ron," I cleared my throat. "Is this ability," I gestured to Marmi, "to see spirits – is it new to you? You know, since your near-death incident?"

"There was no near-death about it. I was as dead as they get. You were there – you saw it."

Yes, I was there, but I didn't know if he remembered himself. "So you remember talking to Marmaduke and then deciding to go back into your body?"

"Not at first I didn't. Everything came back to me in the hospital, although I tried to tell myself it was all a bad dream. But when we brought the gift basket by and I saw him here, I knew." Then he lowered his voice, and leaned toward me." Although, on some level, I think I've always known."

"Always known...what?"

"That I was different."

He was different alright. "You mean, you had experiences before you died?"

He nodded vigorously. "From the time I was," he tilted his head back and forth, thinking, "I don't know, very young, I'd see things – people other people couldn't see. Talked to them. When my parents insisted I was a silly boy with a wild imagination, the people went away for a while, but then, a few years ago, I spotted a ghost while showing a house in historic Old Town. When she started talking to me, I knew." He did some more nodding. "I knew." He wrung his hands and blew out a loud breath as if relieved to have spilled the beans. "I really need to get back to the office before Dory misses me. She keeps a tighter leash on me these days than she used to."

I did a quick survey around. "Moonflower's not being cooperative today. I'm sorry. Do you feel her presence at all?"

He nodded. "Yup. Feel something. Heavy. Big."

Marmaduke had been holding vigil by the door. "My, my," he said, staring at something through the glass door. "The doctor's friend has returned."

At first I thought he meant Moonflower. "She's outside?"

"Not that friend. The young man who has been lingering about the place."

Ron and I stepped toward the door. Sure enough, off in a small cluster of trees stood the kid who'd been following Dr. Callahan.

"He's friends with Dr. Callahan?" Ron asked. "That's strange."

"They're not friends, he's been stalking Dr. Callahan. I'm afraid he's casing the office."

"Oh, I don't think he has a criminal nature. That's Jina's boyfriend, Jonathan."

Aha. Now we were getting somewhere. Excited, I grabbed Ron's arm. "You're sure about that?"

He bobbed his head some more. "Sure as sure can be. She called him Johnny and he pretended to hate it, but he actually loved it. He had it bad for her. Used to surprise her at the office – stopping by to bring her a snack or some candy."

Johnny. That's what Moonflower called Dr. Callahan. Finally things were beginning to make a little more sense. Surely, then, Moonflower was the ghost of Jina Bhandari. Although, why she called herself Moonflower was still a mystery.

"Ron," I gave him a sweet smile. "Can you help me with one more thing before you go back to work?"

"Will it be quick?"

"Won't take more than five minutes of your time, I swear."

Afraid that Jonathan would take off running the way he had earlier in the week, I asked Ron to make an introduction. I wanted the event to appear as natural and unplanned as possible to avoid any possibility that Jonathan would flee the scene. He could be the very answer to all of my problems. Well, they were actually Dr. Callahan's problems, which by default, had become my problems.

We left the office chatting like two old friends. We walked down the little sidewalk that led to the front of the building, as if we were heading toward his office and the mailbox. I brought the mailbox key along just to make it seem more legit. Ron smiled and waved at Jonathan all very friendly-like, and gestured for him to join us. I sweated a few bullets when Ron waved Jonathan over. Acting didn't come naturally to Ronald Ellison. And Jonathan was excessively cautious. But finally, the kid ambled over to the corner where we stood.

"Hey, Mr. Ellison," he mumbled, eyeing us warily. He brushed a few strands of his dirty blond hair away from his forehead. "How have you been?"

"Oh, you know. Good." Ron stuttered a little uncertainly. "Good as can be. Um, this is my friend..." He'd forgotten my name.

I stepped in to assist. "Sophie." I stuck my hand out to shake Jonathan's. I wouldn't say we shook hands so much as I pumped his very limp excuse of an appendage. He obviously wasn't very accustomed to the social grace. Either that or he was scared out of his wits. Which might have been the case. His palm was very sweaty, but then again it was nearly a hundred degrees outside.

Ron snapped his fingers. "Sophie! That's it. Sorry. The heat is getting to me I think." After a moment of awkward silence, Ron clued in that his job wasn't done. "Oh, Sophie works for Dr. Callahan in Suite A. He purchased the unit from Jina's father a few months ago."

The fact that Jonathan's face didn't change in the slightest told me that he was already well aware of that detail.

I played the empathy card. "Ron has told me a lot about Jina," I said. "I'm so sorry. It sounds like she was a really wonderful and sweet person."

Poor Jonathan's eyes actually grew glassy as tears welled up in them. "She was."

"It must be hard."

"Yeah."

My heart was breaking for this poor kid. "You both must have been pretty scared. The idea of becoming a parent, at any age, is intimidating, but probably especially frightening for the two of you."

Jonathan's expression flashed from sad to confused. His eyes widened, his brow crunched. "I'm, um...I don't know...parent?"

So he didn't know that Jina was pregnant or how she'd died, apparently. He must not have been on good terms with her family. The whole thing was just so tragic.

I'd taken Ron by surprise as well. "She was going to have a baby?"

Jonathan started to sway like he might faint. I managed to get an arm around him at the same time that Dory hollered from her end of the sidewalk. "Ronald? What are you doing down there? You have the Tucker house to show!"

"Be right there!" He shrugged apologetically. "Duty calls. Are you, um, going to be okay here?"

"Yeah, I think so," I told him. I bolstered Jonathan a little more. "You're not looking so good. Let me take you to my office and get you a cold glass of water. You can cool down a few minutes. I'm really sorry if I surprised you there. I just assumed you knew."

"Surprised. Yeah. Surprised. Water would be good."

Without meaning to, I'd managed to get Jina's boyfriend into the office. It would be very interesting to see if she came out of hiding for him.

Once I had him resting in a chair in the reception area, I grabbed a cup from the kitchen and filled it with water from the cooler.

"You are a tricky one, aren't you? Bringing the young bloke in here. Do tell – what is your plan now?" Marmaduke asked with the excitement of a young school girl who'd just stumbled onto a bit of juicy gossip.

I whispered as low as I could, making a zipper motion with my fingers across my mouth. "No talking. Just watch."

"Oh, you do know how to take the fun out of things, don't you?"

I shot him a glare to send my point home: *Zip it, Marmi.* Back to the reception area I hustled, full cup in hand. "Here you are, Jonathan. This should help."

Jonathan reached up with shaking hands to take the cool drink. I felt bad for upsetting him. He gulped the water quickly, then shoved the cup back at me. "You're sure she was pregnant?"

While keeping an eye out for Moonflower's appearance, I set the cup on the counter, then sat in the chair next to the boy. "She was definitely pregnant. You didn't know?"

He shook his head.

I rested a comforting hand on his knee. "Do you know how she died?"

A tear fell onto his plaid shorts. He wiped at his nose. "No one in her family would talk to me. My mom asked around and someone finally told her they thought it was a stroke."

"It was an aneurism related to the pregnancy. Were you the...I know it's awfully forward of me to ask, but do you think you were the father?"

More tears fell. It was all I could do not to just wrap my arms around him and hug him tight. He managed a nod finally and he wiped his nose again. I stood to get him a tissue from behind my desk.

Marmaduke didn't abide by my order to stay silent. "This is bloody awful. Did they even let him attend the funeral?" When I snuck a quick peek, I think I detected him sniffling too. Who knew ghosts could cry? Marmaduke's question was a good one though. Maybe it would help draw out some more information.

"Closure often helps in these sorts of situations. Were you at least able to say goodbye to her at the funeral?"

"She was Hindu – well, at least her family was – so I think she was cremated. But I don't know for sure. Closure? Huh. I don't think so."

He wiped his eyes and blew his nose. If I wanted to figure out why she insisted her name was Moonflower, I was just going to have to go out on a limb. "Ron told me that you had a nickname for her...Moonflower, was it?" I cringed inwardly, wondering if the bait would catch a nibble.

He lifted his head and gave me a puzzled look. "Nickname? No."

Darn.

"But," he said a second later, "it was her favorite flower. Her mother grows them in her garden every summer."

There we go.

"Do you think I could get another cup of water?" he asked.

"Sure thing." When I got up to grab the cup, who should I spy hovering mid-air over the desk, but the one and only Jina Moonflower.

"Well, hello again," whispered Marmaduke.

I'd barely had time to register that the trouble maker had finally reappeared when I heard the door open. Spinning around, I caught sight of Jonathan making a dash for it again. The door slammed shut before I could finish my plea. "Jonathan! Come back!" When I turned back around, his dead girlfriend was gone.

Let me rephrase that – she'd disappeared from my sights. She was very much present. The hair on my arms stood on end as the lights flickered once, then twice. "I'm sensing a disturbance in the force," I told Marmaduke.

"The force of what?" he asked, apparently confused by my movie reference. Ghosts don't get to see a lot of movies.

A stack of files lifted straight up off the top of a filing cabinet, hovered for a brief moment, then flew across the room, slamming onto the opposing wall. Papers dispersed like confetti.

"I'm not liking this, Marmi."

For the first time since I've known Marmaduke, he actually looked scared. Something had upset him. "I'm not sure what your 'Force' is, but there is something very, very disturbing occurring on my plane of existence." Like the lights, Marmi flickered off and then on again. The phone rang, startling me.

I answered, only to be jolted by the sound of Moonflower's horrendous wailing in my ears. The minute I slammed the receiver back into its cradle, it rang again. Even though I was suspicious and wary, I lifted it to my ear – more wailing. While replacing the handset a second time, items started flying from my desk at lightning speed. If I didn't get out of there, I'd certainly take a hit.

"Let's get out of here!" I shouted to Marmi while grabbing my purse. I ducked to avoid a collision with an errant brochure holder.

He wasn't arguing. "That certainly is the best idea you have had all day!"

With the door closed behind me in record time, I turned the deadbolt and dashed to my car. I was buckled up and speeding out of the parking lot when Marmi appeared in the seat next to me. "If only I was in possession of a physical body right now. I could use a pint of ale."

CHAPTER THIRTEEN

Marmaduke had the right idea. Since my bank account was enjoying a higher balance thanks to the paycheck, I stopped at the grocery store near my house. There are three things in this world that always calm me down: a cold beer, Stouffer's macaroni and cheese, and Hershey's chocolate with almonds. I stocked up on my comfort foods, then went home and stuffed myself on the mac & cheese and chocolate. I followed the feast with a beer, then fell asleep reading the People magazine I'd picked up as a guilty pleasure.

I woke up Saturday morning with Uno cuddled against the back of my legs and me wondering what the heck I'd gotten myself into. Normal people get up and go to jobs that may not excite them, but at least they're not dodging the wrath of a poltergeist with identity issues.

Booting up my dinosaur of a computer, I searched the online job finder site – the same one that led me to Dr. Callahan. The Stephens City PD had openings. Should I go back, crawling on my hands and knees, begging them to re-hire me? That would mean working with Shane again. Nah. Scratch that. Save that option for the desperation file.

Someone was in need of a smoothie maker at Smoothie Queen. Not a dream job, to be sure, and my boss would probably be some pimply high school kid with a Nazi complex. Scratch that.

A car wash supply company was in need of a bookkeeper – experience required. Scratch that.

A family was in need of a nanny immediately for toddlers aged two and four. Well, kids weren't my strong suit, but I could learn. Must speak fluent French. Scratch that.

Oh look, the ad for Dr. Callahan's job for a receptionist was still there. Odd that no one else had called for an interview. Well, if I gave him my notice, at least he wouldn't have to place it all over again.

Sigh.

I banged my head on the keyboard from frustration. A frustration that was spiraling quickly into a deep depression. I stood up just long enough to fall back down onto my bed in a fit of dramatic melancholy. This disturbed Uno's slumber, who shook himself out then slinked off to his own less shaky cardboard box bed. His departure left me feeling all the lonelier. "Marmi?" I called out.

"You rang?" He appeared, sitting on the edge of the bed.

"Tell me what to do."

"Could you elaborate? Expand your thoughts. Flesh out, as a writer might say, the intent of your request?"

"This job is too much."

"I'd hardly call that a brazen attempt at elaborating. In fact, I would call that a failed attempt. However, I am nothing if not a man of insight, so I will dive into this murky pool with you and offer an observation. I do not believe it is the job that you find overwhelming, but rather a singular element, which, in actuality, is not a component of the employment at all."

"Yeah. I didn't understand anything you just said."

"The beastly ghost is your problem, not the position you hold within Dr. Callahan's business structure."

"She's a real problem alright. I'm torn. Half of me is relieved that I didn't have to go to work today and deal with her. That tells me that I should just cut my losses, quit, and find a different job. Preferably a ghost-free job. They do exist. But then, the other half of me is sad, because I really like Cal. I mean, Dr. Callahan. As an employer, that is."

"Oh, you like him far better than just an employer. You are smitten, there is no doubt."

"I know, right? And then I start to think I like him too much and I've only been working there less than a week and it's just too crazy for me to be falling for my boss, especially this early on. I've already made a fool of myself once with him. I'm lucky he wants to keep me on."

"I have said it once, and I will say it again: he's just as keen on you as you are on him."

"You think? I do feel it. Sort of. Sometimes." I curled up in a ball. Curling up in a fetal position always helps counter the crushing effect of the world collapsing in on me, which is what I felt like at that very moment. Too many variables. Somehow, considering that Cal – Dr. Callahan – might be romantically interested in me made matters worse, not better. Because then, if I followed that road toward its logical course, there was always the complication of what would happen if we did explore a relationship, but then it went sour. As relationships do. I was living proof that breakups happen quite frequently. The room started to feel like it was spinning. I clamped my eyes shut. "I'm going back to sleep."

"Yes, well, not confronting life is always another way to go."

I pulled my pillow from the top of the bed and pressed it tight over my head. A couple more hours of not confronting was just what I needed. I felt badly snubbing Marmaduke when I was the one who called him for help, but sometimes a girl's gotta do what a girl's gotta do. I would apologize later.

A ringing doorbell roused me from my morning nap, which had been light and fitful at best. Stomping angrily to the front door, fully expecting an inane magazine salesman or neighborhood watch representative, I was surprised to see Mrs. Wiley through the peephole. I didn't remember giving her my address.

She knocked again while I worried about opening it, since I was still in my pajamas. My worry over appearing rude overruled my concern for my appearance, and I flipped the knob lock, turned the deadbolt and slid the chain guard free.

"Hi, Mrs. Wiley," I said, peeking through a thin opening. "I'm, uh, not exactly dressed for company." I stepped back, opening the door wide enough for her to enter, but hiding behind the door itself in case neighbors were passing in the hallway. "Let me go get dressed. Can you close the door behind you?"

"Don't worry about impressing me, Sophie."

Running back to my bedroom, I slipped out of my pajama bottoms and into a pair of shorts, then threw a t-shirt over my tank. "What time is it?" I called while checking my hair in the mirror.

"A few minutes after noon. Is that too early?" She called back.

"No, no, no," I said, closing my bedroom door behind me and feeling a little more put together. "But how did you know where I lived?"

Mrs. Wiley was standing between my dining area and living room, but since my apartment is so small, they're practically one and the same. She wore a pair of khaki colored Bermuda shorts and a peach and blue plaid sleeveless cotton collared shirt. Her red, wavy hair was pinned up on her head leaving her shoulders bare. Her makeup was perfect for a summer day and quite honestly put me to shame. I was often inclined to pass up on the blush and mascara on weekend days.

She carried keys in her hand, but no purse.

In response to my question, she grinned and winked. "A little Brit told me." She jangled her keys. "You have a very concerned friend there. I'm not sure I've ever met a spirit so eager to help someone to whom they weren't connected before death. It's the oddest thing." She jangled the keys a second time. Weird habit she had. "I saw a coffee shop right around the corner from here. Would you like to go chat over a cool drink?"

I really liked this woman. She seemed like more than just a good mother – she seemed very genuine. And she understood my predicament better than most people. "Sure," I said, my mood lifting. "Let me get my wallet."

The Coffee Grinder was right around the corner from my apartment – less than twenty steps once you landed on the sidewalk outside of my building. I hadn't ventured in for the longest time since I'm not a coffee drinker, but one day I wandered in, enticed by some yummy looking cookies in the window. That's how I discovered that they made more than just coffee. My favorite drink was a tall iced raspberry lemonade, which I sipped on as Mrs. Wiley and I sat at a small table in the far corner.

"Tell me about your spiritual history, Sophie. How long have you been able to communicate with spirits?"

I winced, not from the question, but from the pain of a minor brain freeze. "Uh...hmm. Good question." I thought back. Way back. "When I was two years old or so, we moved into a house over on Lily Lane. Or maybe it's Lily Street... off of Third Street on the west side of town. From my earliest memories there, I had a friend – a little boy named Wally. For the longest time I didn't even know he wasn't real, but my parents kept laughing and telling everyone about my imaginary friend. As I got older and made other friends who couldn't see Wally, I knew something was up. At some point, I don't know, maybe when I was around six or seven – I was in grade school by then – my mom told me I needed to grow up and stop 'playing pretend' with Wally. And soon after that, I don't have any other memories of him. And I don't remember ever seeing or talking to a ghost again until I met Marmaduke in a bar."

"And what were those circumstances?"

"What do you mean?"

"What was happening at the time? Were you there having a good time with friends or were you alone waiting for friends?"

"Oh, I was alone. My boyfriend had stood me up. We had plans to meet there, then go see a movie after."

She nodded her head as if that meant something significant to her.

"Why?" I asked.

"Sensitive people – people like yourself – are especially open to communication with or from those on the spirit plane during times of stress or peaked emotional activity. It's a gift that's usually very apparent in children, so your story about Wally doesn't surprise me at all. Let's put it this way: your story is common among mediums."

"I'm not a medium."

"By definition, you are. You speak with those in the spirit realm. That's a medium."

"I don't send them into the light or anything."

She laughed. "You've been watching too much television."

"Is there a way to turn off certain spirits, because this Moonflower Jina girl is about to send me over the deep end."

"Marmaduke said you know more about her. What exactly have you learned?"

I summarized the information I'd gleaned from my drunken encounter with Shane along with what Jonathan had told me. She raised an eyebrow when I'd finished. "It sounds to me like she's not entirely sure of who she is. She may not even know where she is. Was she a vicious and violent personality when she was alive?"

"I don't think so. I mean, I've never asked the question specifically, but Ronald told me once that she was a very sweet girl. I think he would have said something."

She slurped the last of her iced drink. "Could you ask him? We should find out for sure. And I'd like to talk to this Jonathan. In the meantime, I should probably try to communicate with her myself." She placed a comforting hand on mine. "Dr. Callahan shouldn't lose a good receptionist like you because of a disturbed spirit. Monday is a busy day with the boys, but I could come by the office in the evening after their father gets home – say, seven o'clock?"

"Do you still think a witch is involved?"

She shrugged. "I'll be honest, I'm not very knowledgeable in the area, but this is feeling more and more like a case I worked on several years ago, before the boys were born. I was asked to help this woman who was being haunted by a male spirit. He was very possessive of her from the moment he appeared. He wouldn't even talk to me. I had to bring in a psychic-medium on the case to assist me. She was able to sense that someone in the vicinity was tapping into the fifth plane."

"Fifth plane? That sounds ominous."

"It's a little complicated – has to do with planes of existence. Long story short – witchcraft was involved. She was an experienced enough psychic to sniff out right away that the neighboring house was involved. Turns out that the woman who lived there was dabbling in the arts with two friends. They accidentally raised the spirit of a young man who had died in my client's house nearly forty years earlier. You know how baby ducks imprint on the first thing they see when they hatch? Well, that's what he had done. The first person he saw when he returned in spirit form was my client. He imprinted on her."

"So what happened?"

"It took some time, but the amateur witches, once we told them what they'd done, were able to safely reverse the spell."

"Safely? Is there danger involved?"

"Can be. I'm not very versed in the subject, though. Probably should be, but with two active boys, you know...so does seven o'clock work for you?"

"I can stick around. Thank you so much."

She winked and picked up her keys from the table. "Let's hold the thank-yous until we get this thing fixed."

Buoyed by my chat with Mrs. Wiley, I showered, ate, and then bravely picked up the phone to call Dr. Callahan. At the very least, I should let him know that the office was in turmoil when I left on Friday. And I'll admit, I wanted to hear his voice.

I dialed his cell phone, then almost hung up once I heard the ringing. It went to voicemail. Almost relieved, I left a long babbling message about Moonflower's poltergeist blowup and how sorry I was that I couldn't do anything about it and if he needed me to do anything, just, well, give me a call.

When I clicked off, I rapped myself on my head with the phone. "That was the stupidest message you've left, ever!" The phone rang in my hands during my self-admonition. The caller ID read Callahan HU. My heart rate picked up. It was that odd feeling between embarrassment and exhilaration that I vividly remembered feeling the time in the seventh grade when Andrew Rinker called me in response to a love note I'd left in his locker. Only I was way past the seventh grade. Shouldn't I be more in control?

"Hello," I answered, my voice cracking. If only there were a more original way to answer the phone.

"Sophie?"

"Yeah. It's me." Oh good. More originality.

"Did you just call?"

"I did. Did you hear my message?"

"No. I didn't pick up in time, so when I saw your name on the ID, I just called you back. Everything okay?"

"Yeah, yeah. I'm fine. Uh, but, I had a bit of a problem at the office yesterday. Moonflower went on another rampage." I purposely left out the part about inviting Jonathan in.

"Really? Man." He went silent for a minute. Not a fan of awkward silences, I was about to give more information when he spoke again. "Was it bad?"

"Pretty bad. Quite bad. Things flying everywhere. I had to leave. That's why I'm calling. It's probably a mess and I left in such a hurry, I didn't set the alarm. I thought I'd go over today to clean up, but, uh, you know... wanted to make sure it was okay with you first."

"Why wouldn't it be okay?"

"I mean, I just started working for you. It's your office, you know, I didn't want to just show up any old time without at least letting you know." Of course, I didn't actually think he'd mind. I really called just to hear his voice. I imagined his blue eyes that crinkled at the edges when he smiled. Ah geez.

"Sure. Thanks," he said, stirring me from my reverie.

"Right. No problem." Well that conversation was short and sweet. I tried to think of something else to say – to keep him talking – then remembered Mrs. Wiley and the plan for Monday night. "Uh, Dr. Callahan..." A beep in my ear stopped me short.

"Hold on, Sophie, someone's trying to call me..."

Suddenly, panic set in and I decided I didn't want to keep talking. "That's okay," I said quickly. "I'll hang up, you take your call and I'll see you Monday. Ciao!" I clicked off.

Ciao? Did I really just say "Ciao"? Stupid, stupid, stupid.

After a few more minutes of chastising myself, I decided to follow through on the promise to go tidy up the office. Hopefully Moonflower wasn't still at it. I washed and dried my few dirty dishes, made sure Peter Pan and Uno had food and fresh water, then scooted out the door with my keys. Marmaduke appeared just as I was starting up the car. "You weren't planning on going alone, were you?" he asked.

"I was pretty sure you'd show up. You always do when I need you." I flashed him a smile. You're my guardian angel, Marmi."

"I might be a guardian," he huffed briskly, "but I'm no angel."

CHAPTER FOURTEEN

The office was indeed a disaster, but it wasn't as bad as I'd expected. It made me wonder if Moonflower had ended her tirade soon after I shot out of there. Both Marmaduke and I noticed almost immediately a different feeling to the place. The intense presence, that large, oppressive pall that she'd cast the day before was gone. It felt as if she was gone.

"Do you think she's with Dr. Callahan?" I asked Marmi, relieved.

"That is a logical assumption."

I set to work setting chairs upright, hanging pictures back on the wall, organizing papers back into the appropriate folders. Halfway through the job, while down on my hands and knees picking pens up from the floor one by one, a jiggling of the front doorknob startled me. My moment of fear was replaced by delight when Dr. Callahan stepped in. "I came to help," he said.

He wore a yellow shirt that popped brightly against his olive skin. And it turned out the man had a nice pair of legs showing under a pair of plaid shorts. I'm a leg woman. Some women like nice butts; I like nice, long, trim and tone legs, and he had them.

"With the clean-up," he added while I ogled too long. The crinkles around his eyes deepened as his smile widened, and I sighed inwardly.

"Yes. With the clean-up. Right. Thanks."

"Hey, she's my ghost, right? It's the least I can do. I should have offered to do it myself, but I've been...a little distracted." He knelt down and started lifting pens, pencils, paper clips, and sticky notes from the floor with me. "Looks like you're nearly done, as it is."

"Nearly," I said, feeling a little out of breath from the racing heart that kicked in when he arrived. I breathed in deeply and reveled in his scent. I blushed when our hands touched while reaching for the same sticky note.

Ah geez. I was acting far too high-schoolish again. I stood and adjusted my shirt and my attitude. This was my boss, not some cute guy in science class, for crying out loud. "Tell you what," I said. "You get the rest of the things on the floor, and I'll finish putting these files back in order."

He agreed, and in no time we'd put his office back into working order, ready for patients on Monday. That was, if Moonflower didn't show up before then and go ballistic-entity on us again. The thought of Moonflower caused me to realize that she hadn't followed Dr. Callahan in. I couldn't see her, and even better, I couldn't feel her.

"I just noticed," I told him, "that you're alone."

"Usually am," he joked.

"I mean, no Moonflower."

"Yeah. Haven't seen her since yesterday. Great, huh?"

"Is that common? For her to disappear for that long?"

"Nope. From the minute she showed up that morning, she's been practically stuck to me like Super Glue. This is a refreshing change. Maybe yesterday's tantrum, I don't know... sent her back to where she came from or something."

His comment about showing up that morning made me think of Mrs. Wiley's client with the spell-induced ghost. "Did she just appear out of the blue one day?" I asked.

He nodded and stood back up, his hands cupped. "Where should I put these paper clips?"

I held out a blue bowl and had to snicker inwardly that he didn't even know where his own office supplies went. The bits of metal clinked as he dropped them in. "I was here on a Saturday installing some new software to use with my therapy patients. Then I—" He stopped himself short. "I'm sorry, you probably don't care about this, do you?"

"Sure I do. I told you my ghost story, it's about time I heard yours."

Brushing his shorts off, he gave a little laugh. "I suppose I do owe you one, huh?" He tipped his head. "Well, I...what was I doing? Right, I needed an instruction manual that I'd left on the desk up here, so when I came to get it, there she was." He gestured with his hands to the middle of the waiting room. "Just staring at me." His eyes widened. "Scared the you-know-what out of me, I'll tell you."

I tried not to laugh. "What did you do?"

"Sat down. Closed my eyes. Counted to ten. Reopened them. Closed them. Opened. Close, open. Started hyperventilating."

"And you'd never seen her before?"

He raised an eyebrow at me. "I'd remember that."

"Yeah," I chuckled. "I guess you would. What did she say?"

"Remember it very clearly – she said, 'Why am I here, Johnny?'" He rolled his eyes. "I feel sorry for her. I mean, she's a lost soul, right? Or something like that. But Johnny here is glad for the break." He moved around behind the desk near where I stood, and looked like he was about to pick up the appointment book when he caught a glimpse of my binder, which I'd neatly labeled, *Optometrist Project*. He picked that up instead. "What's this?"

"Oh, just a little project I've been working on in my free time."

"Project?"

"I hope you don't think it's too forward of me, but I had an idea for bringing new patients in."

"Really?"

I nodded. "Are you okay with it?"

"I don't know what it is yet."

I took the folder from his hand and opened it to reveal a spreadsheet. "I've been gathering names and addresses of optometrists in and around Stephens City. This list isn't quite done. I'm only to the S's, but then..." I flipped to the next page. "Then I drafted this idea for a letter that we – I mean, you – could send them. Sort of an introduction of who you are, that you're a local developmental optometrist, and that you're here if they ever need to refer someone in need of vision therapy. It's only a draft, of course. When I was done entering the names and addresses into the database, I was going to ask you to look at the letter. Fix it or change it as necessary."

He flipped the pages back and forth, studying them intently. His face was flat and expressionless. My face flushed red from embarrassment that I'd crossed a line I shouldn't have. And just when we were having such a nice time. Finally, just before I decided to apologize and offer to quit, he closed the binder and handed it back to me. The beginning of a smile tugged at the corner of his lips. "You did that for me?"

"Yeah. Well, for us. In case you didn't really get it, I need this job badly. You win, I win, right?"

His smile broadened and my heart skipped a few beats. My knees went wobbly.

"I like it. Let me know when that letter is ready. I'll sign it." His eyes locked onto mine.

I tore my gaze from his to set the binder back down next to the keyboard. "Okay." I collected up the pens and pencils that we'd piled on the desk, and slipped them into the pencil cup, then slid it back into position beside the phone.

Dr. Callahan looked around the entire front office area. "Looks good here. I guess our work is done."

Sadly, it was. "Yeah, I guess so," I sighed.

"Hey," he said. "Are you doing anything tonight?"

I tried not to get too excited. He'd asked that question before. "You didn't find another support group did you?"

He grinned. "I deserve that." Then he leaned against the desk. "No. I thought we could use that Winston's gift certificate tonight."

Outside, I remained cool and composed. Inside, I was dancing a jig. "Oh, okay." I reached over and lifted the steno pad from the far side of the desk, holding it up for him to see. "A working dinner, right?"

"Yes," he said with a nod. "A working dinner. Definitely bring the steno pad." He cleared his throat. "And a pen. What time should I make the reservations for?"

Keep it calm, Sophie. "I don't know... seven?"

"Seven. Seven's good. Seven it is."

I gathered my purse and keys, working hard to keep my excitement concealed. "I'll meet you there then." We walked to the door together and I entered the code on the security keypad.

Dr. Callahan opened the door and we stepped outside. "Save your gas. I'll pick you up. Six forty-five." He locked the deadbolt.

I wasn't going to argue with him. Saving gas money sounded good to me. And more time to spend with him. I hoped he was thinking the same.

❧ ❧ ❧

Marmaduke appeared in the car as I drove home. "So you have a date, do you?"

"You were there the whole time, weren't you?"

"Would you have preferred I be more obvious?"

"No. Although I'm surprised that you weren't – you do like to interfere in my love life."

"I do no such a thing. You cut me to the quick. Besides, I approve of this fellow. I cannot say the same about those others."

"I approve of him too. I'm worried though. What if Moonflower shows up at the restaurant?"

"I suppose it is likely she could make an appearance." He seemed to think about that a minute. "And certainly, she has a history of causing trouble."

"You're supposed to be encouraging me, not making me more anxious."

"Sorry, Sophie. I often misunderstand the modern constructs and rules of friendship. How shall I encourage you?"

"Tell me she won't show up."

"I do not think I can say such a thing with certainty. For, while she has not been present this day, we do not know that she has evacuated this plane entirely."

"You're not helping, Marmi."

He became quiet while I fumed at a stop light, then he disappeared altogether.

"Marmi?"

Remaining invisible, he spoke. "A moment of silence please. I am thinking."

"Okay," I muttered under my breath. Why, oh why, couldn't I have one day without a moody ghost around? I wiped sweat from my forehead and wondered how many paychecks it would take to fix the A/C. I turned up the radio, hoping to find an upbeat tune to shoo away my anxiety. *Witchy Woman.* Ugh. I flipped the radio off and decided that sometimes a person has to make their own attitude adjustment if they want to be happy.

Forget Moonflower. I'd go home, shower, pull that cute little blue dress out of the closet, and make myself positively irresistible. Dinner would be spectacular.

"So," said Marmaduke, appearing in his seat again. "You are not to worry."

"It took you that long to figure out how to be positive?"

"Are we not friends?"

"Yes..."

"Then as your friend, I am here to reassure you that your evening shall be free of ghosts. Literal ghosts anyway. I can not offer immunity from metaphorical ghosts."

"Are you up to something?"

"You can thank me later."

CHAPTER FIFTEEN

Before heading to my apartment, I stopped first at the cute little boutique next to the Coffee Grinder – Julie's Jewels – and splurged on a pair of earrings I'd had my eye on for months. The aqua stones would match the blue dress perfectly. At home, I watched the clock carefully while primping, knowing full well Dr. Callahan would arrive precisely at six forty-five. I will admit that I've never been ready when a date has arrived at my door. It's a fault I'm not proud of. Yet, that night, I was one-hundred percent prepared when my doorbell rang at six-forty-six. Aha. The man was late.

I snatched the steno pad and my clutch purse from the table and opened the door, surprised to see Dr. Callahan holding a bouquet of daisies neatly tied at the stems with a blue ribbon.

Did he know daisies were my favorite flower? And the blue ribbon – surely it was a sign. My heart thumped double-time. I wasn't sure what caused the palpitation – the flowers or Dr. Callahan, who looked particularly dashing in a tan sport coat and white collared shirt open at the neck. I decided it was both.

If I were a more forward woman, and if I didn't think I'd jeopardize my employment status, I would have been inclined to jump his bones, run my fingers through that soft, golden hair, and have my way with him, right on the spot.

Working to hold my smile down to working-dinner-appropriate, I pointed shyly to the bundle in his hands. "I thought this wasn't a date."

"I know," he sputtered, shoving them at me. "There were these kids outside my barber – collecting money for the home-less shelter. They gave me these for donating twenty bucks."

Yes, that was part of the dashing new look. He'd had his hair trimmed. My fingers ached to brush it. Ah geez. Down to earth, Sophie. Come back down to earth.

Ω"Do you like...marigolds?" he asked when I returned happy and content.

His incorrect flower classification made me chuckle. "They're daisies, and yes, I love them. They're actually my favorite flower."

"Not roses?" he asked as I pulled the door closed and locked the deadbolt.

"Roses are overrated. Give me a daisy or a lily any day. I'll bet moonflowers are your favorite."

He laughed loudly while we made our way down the stairs. "Uh – no. Actually, now that I think of it, I don't even know what a moonflower is."

His left hand slipped to the small of my back while he opened the glass entrance door with his right. My body tingled all over. Somehow, he'd been lucky enough to snatch a park-ing spot right in front of the building – not an easy feat on a Saturday in my apartment complex. Sometimes people had to park clear out on the main drag. I silently thanked the god of parking spaces, since my feet weren't generally used to the high heels I'd chosen for the occasion. Summer for me meant flip-flops and flat sandals, not heels.

Dr. Callahan scooted around me to the passenger-side door and opened it for me. Shane had never once opened a car door for me. The smile, that hadn't left my face, widened.

"Thank you, Dr. Callahan. You didn't need to do that though." Yes he did. Yes he did. I loved every minute of it.

"Yeah. You can't call me that tonight."

"Sorry. Force of habit. Cal."

"There you go."

"You sure you don't want me to call you Hiram?" I teased.

He bent his head close to mine when I was positioned in the seat and reaching for the belt. "There is probably only one reason I'd ever consider firing you, and calling me Hiram is it." His face, flat and serious at first, curled adorably into the sweet, crooked smile.

Ah geez, but he was cute.

Once at Winston's the maître d' sat us in a dark and quiet corner, just perfect for not talking business. The plump luxury of the padded, high-back chairs were a far cry from the hard rigidity of the wooden stools at Barney's. No offense to Barney.

Cal cleared his throat and clasped his hands in front of him on the table. "You look really...very nice tonight." Another clearing of the throat. "Pretty, I mean."

"Thank you. So do you." Crap. That came out wrong. He's not pretty. Stupid, stupid, stupid. I shook my head. "That is... uh, you're..." The words weren't forming so I was thankful that the waiter arrived on the scene.

"Would you like to see a wine list, sir?"

Cal turned his attention from the waiter to me. "Do you drink wine?"

I nodded, "Sure."

"What do you like?"

"Sauvignon Blanc?"

"Really? Me too." He turned back to the waiter. "Do you have a bottle of Cloudy Bay, by chance?"

The waiter tipped his head. "We do." He turned on his heels very officiously and left for the wine.

"It's a New Zealand winery. Have you heard of it?"

I sipped from the water that a bus boy had already poured for us. I didn't know anything about wines. Hanging around cops, it had been beer and whiskey or tequila shots for the past couple of years. I'd heard my mother mention a Sauvignon Blanc once, that's why I said it. With my nervous-dry mouth soothed, I eeked out, "No. Do they make good wines?"

He winked. "You'll see."

The waiter made a big production of the opening of the wine, pouring a small bit into Cal's glass, then waiting for Cal's approval. I'll admit it – I was impressed. I was equally impressed with the wine. A nice change. And I felt very elegant sipping from the enormous orbed glass.

Cal and I exchanged smiles. He peeked at me and I peeked at him while the waiter rattled off the evening's chef's specials. He finally decided on the swordfish with orzo pasta and I went with herb roasted chicken and mushroom risotto.

The nice thing about menu-time during a date is that it eases tensions and gives a couple something to talk about. Once the order is placed and the waiter leaves, the real struggle begins. Luckily, we had a fall-back.

I smoothed the dinner napkin in my lap. "So, what's on the agenda for our business discussion this evening?"

He pointed to the pad that I had set under my clutch purse. "Get that steno."

Darn. He really did want to talk business. Oh well. I took a big sip of wine and did as he asked. He pulled a pen from inside his sport coat and handed it to me. "Write this down," he instructed.

I readied the pen over a blank sheet and waited.

"On Monday, I'll need you to order three home therapy kits. I'm down to my last one. Okay, close that pad and put it away."

"That's it?"

"Business is over. Time for us to get to know each other."

"Okay." I approved. "Who goes first?"

"You. Definitely. I'm very boring."

I set the steno aside and handed his pen back. "Oh, my story will probably put you to sleep before your swordfish arrives, but uh, actually, do you mind if I ask a sort of personal question?"

He arched his brows. "What's your definition of personal?"

"How old are you?"

"I get that a lot. I look young for my age. I'm thirty-one."

Excellent. Two years older than me. That worked. "Yeah, I wouldn't have guessed that. You look younger. Usually."

He nodded. "It can be tricky getting parents to trust me. They're afraid I'm fresh out of school and have no idea what I'm doing. You're... let me guess... twenty-nine."

"You should open up shop in a carnival. Want to guess my weight next?"

"Didn't really guess," he said on a shrug and a grin. "Your birth date is on the tax form you filled out for payroll."

"Of course. That makes sense." But he took the time to look and do the math. Good sign.

"And from your social security number, I know you were born around here."

Okay. He really was paying attention. Even better sign. "Stephens City Hospital. Can't get more local than that."

"So you have family here?"

"Not anymore. I take that back. My Grampy is here. Mom and Dad divorced a few years ago. She moved to Phoenix and he moved to Alaska."

"They were as different as their retirement locations?"

"Basically. How about you? Did you grow up here?"

"Yup. Mason Ridge." Stephens City, Mason Ridge, and Wells Corner formed a famous triad of towns that might as well have been one big city. Each had four elementary schools, two middle schools, and one high school.

"Oh? So you went to Mason Ridge High School."

"Go Razorbacks."

"Ha, we whooped your butts the entire four years I was at West Stephens High."

"Now here's what I never understood – there's only one high school in Stephens City. Why is it called West Stephens High?"

"Leaving the option open for an East Stephens High?"

"So you don't have brothers or sisters?"

"I have a brother. He lives in Wells Corner."

"You didn't mention him in your list of local relatives."

"We're not very close."

"That's too bad."

Darn. That was just the kind of conversation killer that I'd hoped wouldn't arrive on the scene. We both took time during the awkward silence to sip some wine when a couple, being escorted to their table by the maître d', spotted Cal and took a detour. The man, whom I deduced was the husband of the pair based on the wedding ring, patted my dinner partner on the back. "Hey, Coach Callahan! How are you?"

Cal twisted around, surprised. He smiled and stood to shake the man's hand. "Mr. Sullivan. Good to see you." He shook the lady's hand as well. She smiled broadly in return.

"Mrs. Sullivan," said Cal. "Um, this is Sophie Rhodes. A friend." They gave me friendly smiles.

"How is Lindsay?" Cal asked the couple.

"She's good," said the dad. "Ready for the game. Listen, we don't want to interrupt you two, just wanted to make sure we said 'Hi.'" He shook Cal's hand again. We'll see you tomorrow."

"Yup, yup," nodded Cal. "Enjoy your dinner."

The Sullivans were walking away when two servers came with our plates, followed by the waiter who instructed them where to set them down. I talked around the servers. "Coach Callahan?" I asked.

"I coach a girls soccer team."

The waiter refilled our wine glasses, which were quite low, then asked us if we needed anything else. I shook my head.

"We're good, thank you," Cal told him.

I dipped my fork into the risotto. "Girls and soccer. I bet that keeps you busy. How old are the girls?"

"Sixth grade right now. I've been with this team of girls for three years. And yes, they do keep me busy. Actually, the girls are great. Hard workers, fun. The parents are great too. A couple of the other coaches have some problem parents, but I'm lucky."

"Why are you seeing them tomorrow? It's not soccer season is it?"

"Just for fun, we're playing a couple of teams over the summer. Gets the girls together, keeps the team spirit high, and they get some practice in."

"Sounds like fun."

"It is. Although, ever since Moonflower has shown up, it's been a little trying. I never put two and two together before, but you're right. She doesn't like me around women. Young or old."

"Speaking of Moonflower – she's surprisingly absent still."

"And I've noticed we're free of Marmaduke too. Thank goodness for small favors."

"While we're on the subject, I wanted to talk to you about Mrs. Wiley."

"Mrs. Wiley?" He made a face while trying to place the name. "Oh! The mother of the twins. Nice lady."

"Right. She is. Really nice, actually. And she's a medium."

"You mean, as opposed to a large or extra-large?"

"A medium – a person who communicates with spirits."

"She actually put that down on the information sheet?"

"No, she handed me her card." I fished through my clutch, since I'd slipped it in there purposely to show him, and handed it over when I found it. "She knew Moonflower was a problem the minute she stepped into the office the other day."

He inspected the card in his hand. "You think we should call her?"

"Actually, I already did. She, uh, she's willing to come by Monday after hours to see if she can talk with Moonflower and..." I realized I was leaving out a huge part of the story. "Let me back up a little. There's more you should know."

I took him all the way back to the resurrection of Ronald Ellison, mentioned the information the Ellisons gave me about Jina Bhandari, through my first conversation with Mrs. Wiley, on to the reason for my drunken escapade at Barney's with Shane, threw in the introduction to Jina's boyfriend and the father of her unborn baby, Jonathan, and finished up with Mrs. Wiley's visit to my apartment and her willingness to help tap into Jina/Moonflower's frequency. The speech was long and uninterrupted. I needed a big swig of ice water to hydrate my dry mouth afterward. I eyed Cal's reaction over the rim of my glass while I gulped.

After a significant amount of time without a response from him, I decided to fish for an acknowledgment, good or bad. "Are you okay with all of this?"

He remained motionless, but finally spoke. "You mean, I didn't save Ronald Ellison's life?" The disappointment on his face was heartbreaking.

Here I was worried that he didn't care for all of my self-directed investigative work, and he was still hung up on the introduction to my long and sordid tale. I suppressed a smile and winced instead. "Not really, no. But Dory Ellison doesn't know that. She's still very grateful."

"Grateful for nothing. So basically, I did nothing more than swap spit with a dead man who brought himself back to life."

"Isn't it the thought that counts?"

"You're sure that Moonflower is the ghost of this Jina Bhandari?"

"Everything fits. She calls you Johnny, and that's what she called her boyfriend. Her favorite flower was the moonflower, and she said her name was Moonflower."

"It's very nice of Mrs. Wiley, but I don't know..." he scanned the restaurant. "Maybe we won't need her after all. This would have been the kind of thing Moonflower – uh, Jina? – would have shown up for. Maybe seeing her boyfriend in our office was just what she needed and she's off bothering him now."

I shrugged. He could have been right. But I had left out a key piece of information, and while it was true that Jina Moonflower might have moved on, I wouldn't feel right if I didn't mention it anyway. "There's one other little thing I forgot to mention," I said hesitantly.

He raised his eyebrows questioningly.

"What are your thoughts on witchcraft?"

It took two glasses of water and a promise that I wouldn't talk about witches, but eventually, Cal's sudden coughing fit subsided. We ordered dessert and managed to find our way back to some enjoyable and enlightening conversation. I learned that he also enjoyed hiking, although he didn't find the time for it as he'd like, and on our drive home, he found out about my love for animals and desire to be trained as a wildlife rehabilitator some day.

At my apartment building, he walked me up to my door. I had no idea if I should ask him in or not. If this were a date with anyone who wasn't my employer, and I liked him the way I liked Cal, I would have. But this was different. I decided rather than hedge the subject, I'd attack it square on. I pulled the key from my purse. "I'll be honest, I don't know if I should ask you in or not..."

He shook his head. "I have to get up early for that soccer game tomorrow. Need to go get some shut-eye."

That was easy. Disappointing, but easy.

"Okay," I nodded. I slipped the key into the lock, then looked into those blue eyes.

The crooked smile appeared and he leaned in close, dropping his voice to a sexy near-whisper. "It's soap."

Those stomach-butterflies that were noticeably absent when talking to Shane, now arrived in a swarm. "What?" I asked, enjoying the proximity of his lips to mine. If he came any closer, kissing them would be required. Or possibly I'd just nuzzle into the crook of his inviting neck. Oh man, nuzzling would be really nice. My hormones kicked in, warming areas that hadn't been warmed in a while.

"I don't wear cologne." He tilted his head ever so slightly, making that potential kiss even easier, if one of us were so inclined. "You're smelling the soap that I use."

My face flushed hot at the reminder of my excessive fawning over his fragrance. Embarrassed, I broke his stare and looked at my hands. "I am, uh, so sorry for... coming on so strong, you know. The other night. It was... the whiskey talking."

"I hope it wasn't only the whiskey." He turned my face back to look at his. "I liked what you had to say."

Ah geez.

He kissed my cheek. "Good night."

"Uh-huh." I sighed.

He departed down the stairs, but turned and gave me one more smile before disappearing.

Good night.

I'm fairly sure I floated into my apartment and right over to my couch where I plopped down and hugged a throw pillow, smiling.

Peter Pan was already out and running in his wheel. He stopped for a minute, gazed at me with his bulging black eyes, wiggled his little whiskers, then went back to running. I sat up and looked into the cage, desperate to tell someone what a wonderful night I'd had. "Peter – he's just so nice and cute and... nice. He donates money to the homeless and coaches girls soccer. I think he might just be perfect."

Peter loves me, I know, but he didn't really care. He needed exercise after all. Uno was digging in his litter box ready to do his business, so the time was wrong for opening a conversation with him.

"Marmaduke?" I called out. Marmi would be glad for me. At least, I hoped he would be. "Marmi?" I called again.

Hmm. That was odd.

I stood and called into the air again. "Marmi? Are you there?"

Well, if he was there, he wasn't showing himself, and he certainly wasn't talking to me.

I went to bed, still happy about my evening with Cal, but quite frankly, more than a little worried about my friend and where he'd disappeared to.

CHAPTER SIXTEEN

The doorbell woke me from a strange and somewhat disturbing dream about Moonflower and Marmaduke, yet the moment my eyes were open, I could barely remember the events of the dream – just the emotion of it. Fear.

I stumbled to the door, thankful to be released from the dream, but irritated with whomever was ringing the bell. A blurry peek through the peep hole erased any annoyance I had experienced. My visitor was Cal. I smiled and pulled the door open, forgetting I wore nothing more than a very skimpy pair of pajama shorts and a tank top.

"We won!" he said brightly, holding up a McDonald's bag and a cup holder with two drinks inserted. "Care to celebrate with me?"

"What time is it?"

"Ten fifteen. Too early?"

"Not for soccer coaches, apparently. Let me, uh, get something on... stay there." I ran to my room, pulled a robe from the closet and tied it on. Returning, I gave him the green light to come in, pulling the door open wide. "What did you get me?"

He unloaded the bag onto my small round dining table. Two wrapped breakfast sandwiches and two orders of hash browns. Or, at least what McDonald's calls hash browns.

"Well," he explained, "it was tricky, because I wasn't sure if you were a vegetarian since you're an animal lover, but then I remembered you had chicken for dinner last night, so I got you a chicken biscuit. Does that work?"

"Sure."

"And caffeine-laced soda – Coke."

We both pulled out chairs and sat. "A breakfast fit for a queen." I stuck a straw into the soda lid and sipped heartily. "What was the score? Did you annihilate the opposition?"

"Crushed them, I'm proud to say. Nine to zero."

"My stomach thanks them. And you." I chomped down into the juicy biscuit sandwich, making sure to wipe away any errant crumbs hanging around the edges of my mouth, then sipped some more soda.

He took a bite of his McMuffin and looked around the apartment while he chewed. After a swallow, he raised an eyebrow. "Where's Marmaduke?"

"Good question." I called out again. "Marmi? Are you there?" Nothing. My tummy felt like it was starting to reject the chicken biscuit. "Hmm." I tried again, putting a sing-song twist on the summons. "Marmi, come out, come out wherever you are." No sound other than that of Cal sipping his hot coffee. I put the sandwich back down on the wrapper. "He wasn't around last night, either," I said.

"Maybe he and Moonflower – Jina? – took a little vacation together. I haven't seen her for a while either."

"This isn't like Marmaduke, though. He's usually around if I call."

"Trust me, not like my ghost either. She's been like a piece of toilet paper stuck to the bottom of a shoe that you just can't shake off."

I gave it some thought, then realized that Marmaduke was probably just giving me some space to get to know Cal. He had promised me things would go well, and they had. Really well. In fact, it made sense that he was probably around and just keeping quiet since Cal was there now. Deciding all was probably just fine, I polished off the remaining bit of sandwich and slurped from the soda cup until all that was left was ice. "Don't get me wrong," I said, rolling the sandwich wrapper and throwing it back into the McDonald's bag. "I love that you came this morning, but..."

He anticipated my question. "Why am I here?"

"Yeah."

He wadded his sandwich wrapper, sending it into the bag behind mine. "I had a good time last night."

I smiled. "Me too."

He turned in his chair, his knees touched mine. "I kind of didn't want it to end."

"Me either."

"Do you ever go hiking?"

Never hiked in my life. "Uh, you know, I have, uh, hiked..." I shook my head. I was going to try to finesse it and seem like I was Ms. Outdoors, but I'd been there done that with pretending to be something I wasn't just to be with a man. I was almost thirty – time just to be myself. "Honestly? No."

"Oh."

"But I'll try anything once." I reconsidered that claim. Better not open the door to the strange and kinky. I didn't know him that well. "Uh, within reason, that is."

"I thought we could go up to Ridge Falls Park. They have some amazing hiking trails there. I'm surprised you've never been there since you grew up around here."

"I said I'm not a hiker. I didn't say I've never been to Ridge Falls Park." The fact of the matter was, Ridge Falls Park had a very famous boulder that overlooked the falls. People called it the kissing rock. I'd done some time with more than one boyfriend on the kissing rock. It was a good place for making out, that was for sure. But I wasn't bringing that up just yet. Later maybe...

He scooted his chair back and stood. "I was being a little presumptuous, but I packed water bottles and a lunch already."

"Then I can't say no, can I? I don't have hiking boots though."

"We can stick to the easy trails. Just wear tennis shoes."

"Those I have."

Thankfully, a cool mass of air had swept in overnight, turning down the heat dial from the oppressive high nineties to more comfortable low eighties with virtually no humidity. I was pleased from a comfort perspective, not to mention that I wouldn't look like I'd taken a detour through a car wash by the end of our hike.

Outside of the car in the parking lot at Ridge Falls Park, Cal threw a backpack over his shoulder and pointed the way to a trail that began at the far end of the lot near a large picnic pavilion. "We'll take that one. Founder's Trail. It splits off part of the way up to a more difficult trail, but if we stay on Founder's we'll still find a couple good spots with good views of the falls."

"You're the experienced one. You lead, I'll follow."

"I'm surprised, with your interest in wildlife, that you don't hike. It's a great way to see wild animals in their natural environment."

"Remember, I'm just in the desiring-to-be-a-rehabilitator phase. Still have a way to go. It's a long road from interest to actually doing the training." I was already huffing and puffing and we'd only traveled a few yards on the trail.

"You should do that. The research I mean. Were you one of those kids that came out of the womb loving animals?"

"I don't know about that early. But my first word was kitty. And I went on to beg my parents endlessly for pets." I paused to catch my breath. "This is the easy trail?"

He laughed. "The payoff is just around the corner. Trust me, the workout is worth it. How many pets did they let you have?"

"Two dogs, two cats, and a bearded dragon." Feeling rested enough, I started moving again, Cal following my lead.

"A bearded dragon. Don't they live a long time? Like a hundred years or something?"

I shook my head and giggled. "I think you're thinking of sea turtles. Bearded dragons only live to be about ten. Unless you own two cats who manage to get into his habitat and scare him into cardiac arrest."

Cal made a face. "They didn't have him for dinner afterwards, did they?"

"Luckily, no." I shook my head. "It was a sad day when we buried Abraham Lincoln. How about you? Did you have pets?"

"No. My mom had allergies. Not to the animals themselves – to the work involved. She didn't trust me or my sister to pull our weight in the care and feeding. I take that back. I had a hamster. For a day. That's uh... a long story." His face brightened and he pointed. "Here's one of the lookouts." He placed his hand at the small of my back and guided me to a flat piece of ground to our right that lay in the opening between some trees. My entire body tingled at his touch. Then I gasped at the view. The view from kissing rock had nothing on this one. From the higher vantage point, we could see the full expanse of the river as it gushed over the massive boulders around the bend.

"It's gorgeous!"

"You should see it at sunrise on a clear day." He pointed to the other side of the falls. "The sun comes up over that ridge and it looks like the trees are on fire. It sounds trite, but the only way I can describe it is that it takes your breath away."

I turned to see his face when a wall of bright white light flashed in front of me. The blinding light was accompanied by an ear-piercing screech.

Instinctively, I covered my ears with my hands and squeezed my eyes shut. The ground felt like it was crumbling beneath my feet and nausea overcame me like a wave pounding the shore. "Oh, crap!" I screamed. "What is that?"

Cal pulled me back from the lookout while I was bent over.

"What's wrong?" His voice was muffled with my hands still trying to shut out the screech, which had gone as quickly as it came.

Hesitantly, I opened my eyes and pulled my hands from my ears. "Didn't you hear that awful noise? See that light?"

"I didn't see or hear anything. Here." He helped me stand upright, then tipped my chin to move my face toward his. "I want to see your eyes." He looked into my eyes seriously and intently; with professional care. "Do you get migraines?"

"No. Never."

"What happened?"

"There was this flash of light – bright, bright light – and at the same time a horrible... screeching noise. Sharp, high pitched, and fast. Like someone turned it on and off again with a switch."

I was just catching my breath when it happened again. "Oh, geez!" I screamed, doubling over and falling to my knees. This time, while the light flashed, the tiniest bit longer than the first, a vague outline formed in my vision. A tree? A person? It was hard to tell. Then it and the sound were gone and I found myself on the ground, pine needles pressing painfully into my naked knees.

Cal was on his knees next to me rubbing my back. "Are you okay?"

"It's gone. Oh, this is... it isn't fun. Make it stop."

"Tell me when you think you can stand again. We should get back to the car."

I waited a second for the nausea to pass, then let him pull me up. We turned and slowly started making our way back down the path toward the parking lot.

"Lean on me if you need to," Cal said.

"I'm fine now. I think."

He pulled the backpack off his shoulder and handed me a bottle of water. "Drink. Maybe you're dehydrated."

Water sounded good, and I did gulp it down, but I didn't think it was dehydration. Truthfully, I was becoming very embarrassed. "I'm sorry to ruin the hike. Maybe I'm coming down with something."

He felt my forehead. "You don't feel feverish."

With each step that we made it closer to the car, I was more and more thankful for another moment free from that agonizing pain to my eyes and ears. In all my life, I'd never had such a grueling experience, as short-lived as it was. And I was praying it would never happen again. Momentarily, remembering how my Grammy, my mother's mother, had died of a stroke, I panicked. I grabbed Cal's arm. "Do you think I had a stroke?"

"I'm an eye doctor, not a neurologist, but I don't think so. Your speech was never slurred. Hold your arms over your head."

I stopped walking and did as he said. He gave me a visual once over and shook his head. "I don't think it's a stroke. It's very possible you're having migraine symptoms. I want to take you back to the office and get a look at your optic nerve." Nice, caring and in control!

How sweet was Cal? Shane would have told me that he wanted to take me home and screw me silly, because in his mind, sex solved everything. This was a refreshing change. Someone who cared. I was feeling all silly and wilty – hard to tell if it was Cal or side-effects from my odd attack.

I gulped down the rest of the water. "Back to the office. Optic nerve. Sounds good."

Five minutes into the ride back to Stephens City and the Stephens City Office Park, I felt as healthy and normal as ever.

"You're right," I said, feeling very happy and comfortably cozy sitting next to Cal in his car. "Maybe I was just dehydrated. I feel fine now."

"I still want to look at that optic nerve. It will make me feel better."

I smiled. He wanted me to feel better. I sighed inwardly. There's nothing more romantic than a man who wants to take care of a woman. A girl can be as independent as she wants and as in charge as she wants, but it's always a knee-buckler when a man is strong enough and willing to take care of her. Of me.

My cell phone jingled in my purse. I recognized the number right away. "It's Mrs. Wiley," I told Cal.

"Hello?" I answered.

"Sophie, this is—"

Before I could hear the rest of what she had to say, the flash of light returned, brighter, even more intense, followed by a quick sharp image of a pained Marmaduke. I heard him wail, then the image was gone. I was aware of Mrs. Wiley's voice in my ear again. "...he needs our help."

I could fill in the blanks. I didn't need to ask her to repeat what I'd missed.

I pulled the phone from my face for a quick moment. "The flashing lights," I told Cal. "It's not my optic nerve – it's Marmaduke. He's in danger."

CHAPTER SEVENTEEN

I yelled into the phone, panicked now. "Mrs. Wiley, what do we do?"

"I'm sensing a powerful epicenter of energy emanating from Dr. Callahan's office. We should meet there."

"We're actually almost there now. We're pulling into the parking lot." The minute we turned the corner, I caught sight of Jonathan and the strangely-behaving army jacket girl who'd been in the office earlier that week. They stood together about thirty feet from the door of the office, as if in a trance. "Jina's boyfriend is here," I told her.

"Whatever you do, don't go into the office until I get there. I'm just two or three minutes away myself. Find out what you can from the boyfriend. Maybe he's hiding something."

"That's the boyfriend?" Cal asked when I disconnected. "Who's the girl?"

"She's the one I told you came in that day pretending to want an eye exam. When I thought they were thieves casing the place."

He parked, and when I put one foot out of the car onto the pavement, I suffered another attack of bright light and screeching in my ears – the worst yet. More powerful, more painful, longer duration. "Oh, God!" I screamed, grabbing my head, waiting for relief. Cal ran to my side and kept me from falling over. When the event ended and I stopped moaning, he helped me stand upright.

"What the hell is going on, Sophie?"

"I'm not sure. Mrs. Wiley is on her way. All I know is that Marmaduke is in trouble and whatever that trouble is, it's happening there." I pointed to the office.

"I should take you home. Maybe the farther away we get, the better."

I shook my head. "No, Marmaduke needs me. Plus, if distance were a factor, I would have been fine at the falls." I took a deep breath. "Let's talk to Jonathan and that girl to see what they know. It can't be a coincidence that they're here."

Cal held me around the waist in case of another attack. Jonathan and his friend watched us approach them. Their eyes were filled with terror.

"Who's your friend, Jonathan?"

"We didn't mean for any of this to happen," he said, then turned his gaze back to the front door of the office.

Cal and I followed his glassy-eyed stare. Through the glass panes of the door, it was easy to see bright flashes of light as if a lightning storm were going on inside. The Venetian blinds that hung in the four windows along the front wall flopped and whipped about. A low roar rumbled underneath our feet.

I jumped when Marmaduke's pained face flashed in one of the windows.

I turned back to Jonathan, unable to control my anger. "Jonathan, what have you done?"

"It's my fault, not his," said the girl.

"This is Astrid. She... I can't believe this!" He shook his head. "I asked her to."

"To what? Astrid, what did you do?"

"A raising spell. It was supposed to be easy. He was so sad. He missed her so much. My aunt is a witch."

"She gave you the spell?"

"Not exactly. I mean, my great, great, great-something aunt was a witch. I thought I'd just give it a try. Maybe it was in my blood or something."

"The spell. Where did you get the spell?"

"The Internet."

Cal chuckled. I shot him a chastising glare. "This isn't funny!"

He shook his head. "No, no, you're right. It's not funny at all. Scary. Bizarre. The laugh – a nervous one. Sorry. But Internet and witches spells..." He didn't finish the thought. "Never mind. Not funny."

We both looked back at the office in time to see more fireworks from inside, then the flashing image of Jina Bhandari, an expression of fury on her face that caused every hair on my body to stand on end.

"I don't think my insurance covers paranormal storms," Cal uttered under his breath.

Mrs. Wiley's car pulled around from the back of the building and screeched to a stop a few feet away. She stared at the activity in Cal's office while running to where we stood.

"What do we know?" she asked, panting.

"This is Astrid," I answered, pointing to the girl. "She's the culprit. Brought Jina Bhandari's spirit back with a raising spell."

Mrs. Wiley nodded. "That's what I thought. Please don't tell me you got the spell off the Internet."

"We thought she'd appear in front of us, but she didn't. We thought it didn't work. But then I felt this pull one day. I came by and saw her following him." She pointed to Cal.

"We've tried everything to change it. Make it so she could talk to Jonathan."

Mrs. Wiley's face blanched. "What did you try?"

Astrid pulled her head down into her shoulders like a turtle hiding in its shell. "More spells..."

The low rumbling grew louder and louder. Where it appeared that the wind was only originating from inside, small funnels of dirt and mulch arose from the landscaping outside, underneath the windows. And the bushes swayed as if a breeze blew through them, yet I felt no wind at all. A loud crack caused us all to jump and yell.

"What was that?" Jonathan cried out.

"I think lightning hit the building." Cal's right arm was still bent in the air from his reflexive shielding.

"The energy is growing," said Mrs. Wiley. "We need to go inside and stop this if we can."

Cal's eyebrows furrowed deeply. "That does not sound like a good idea."

Another sharp flash buckled me to my knees. The screech was now the intensely high-pitched squeal of fingernails scratching across a blackboard, only a hundred times louder. I screamed loud enough for people ten towns away to hear. It was the only way to keep the pain from ending me altogether.

Then, as suddenly as it began, the squeal ended, but was replaced by Marmaduke's pleas. "Sophie!" he cried out. "Help!"

"Do you hear that?" I yelled, while grabbing Cal's leg.

"You mean your screaming?"

"No! Marmaduke. He's crying out for help."

He pulled me to my feet. "You can't go in there. It's killing you."

I pushed him away, stumbling closer to the office. "I'm going in there. He needs me."

A strong wind brushed past my calves, then migrated higher and higher until I realized that we were being engulfed by a massive funnel cloud. We shielded our eyes from dust and debris. The only way we could hear each other was to yell above the din.

"You're not going in there without me!" Cal turned to Mrs. Wiley. "What do we do when we get in there? Is there a plan? A spell?"

"I'm a medium. Witchcraft isn't my area," she yelled back. "I know a woman, but she's unreachable. I tried on my way here. But I have one idea."

"Does it involve Sophie going through more pain?" he hollered.

"If we don't do something now, she may die with both of those souls in there!"

"I'll do whatever it takes," shouted Astrid. She reached to hold back the hair that blew in her face.

Cal readied his keys. "What if your idea doesn't work?"

"Then hopefully I can at least calm them down through communication."

"And if that doesn't work?"

"Let's cross that bridge if we reach it," shouted Mrs. Wiley, pushing her way into the wind toward the door.

Cal and I followed Mrs. Wiley, and Astrid and Jonathan followed on our heels. The five of us struggled against the force of the wind that seemed to hold us close, yet felt compelled to keep us away. After a couple of tries, Cal was able to force the key into the lock.

"Let me go in first," shouted Mrs. Wiley. He pulled on the door and allowed her to step past him. Oddly, inside, despite the flapping blinds, the wind was barely detectable, but the minute Mrs. Wiley stepped in, items in the room began to levitate.

Chairs, papers, the computer, pens, pencils. Everything. Outside, we strained against the wind gusts. Mrs. Wiley grasped my arm and pulled me in. "Astrid, get in here!" she shouted.

Astrid obeyed and I released a sigh of relief as the intense pounding relented.

Cal stepped in to stand close behind me. He poked me and pointed up where the ceiling should have been. Should have been, because instead of a ceiling, there was only a swirling black storm cloud.

Inside the spinning cloud, Marmaduke and Jina were held in suspended animation. Marmaduke's face was contorted, as if in agony. Jina's eyes were filled with hate.

"Sophie," instructed Mrs. Wiley, "see if you can talk with Marmaduke. Find out what's happening, what's keeping him there." She took Astrid by the hand. "Young lady, you need to listen to me carefully. I'm not sure you'll understand everything I'm about to say, but do your best to do exactly as I say."

Astrid nodded, wide-eyed.

"Why is she stuck up there like that?" Jonathan cried out. "Jina!" he screamed. "Jina, do you hear me?"

His plea made no change. Around they spun, Marmaduke and Jina, like two people in an amusement park ride.

"When anything in the physical or spiritual realms is duplicated precisely, they fall away as if they never existed in the first place. This happens with thought, with emotions, anything. This is why you can dispel an upset by talking about it. What you need to do, Astrid, is duplicate very, very exactly, the original spell. Forget everything you tried after. Put yourself in the moment, imagine where you were, how you felt. Then recreate that moment and that spell absolutely precisely. I can't stress the importance of the duplication here, Astrid. Can you do that?"

Astrid nodded vigorously while Jonathan paced under the black cloud, staring at his beloved Jina.

"Sophie!" Mrs. Wiley chided me. "Marmaduke! I need you talking to him during this. Contact him if you can. The stronger he's attached to you and to this plane, the better his chance of being pulled from whatever this is."

I'd been so caught up in her instruction to Astrid that I'd fallen down on my duty to connect with Marmaduke.

"Are you sure about this?" Cal whispered in my ear.

"I'm sure." I took his hand. "Stay close, okay?"

"I'm not going anywhere."

I saw Astrid close her eyes. I did the same and spoke out to Marmaduke. "Marmi? Are you there Marmi?"

Nothing. My heart sank.

"Try again, Sophie," said Mrs. Wiley. "Astrid, go back to that moment when you cast the spell. Feel what it was like. How it smelled. Was it warm or cold?"

I found the circumstances distracting, to say the least, but I gave it another go, boosted by the gentle, encouraging squeeze of Cal's hand. "Marmaduke? It's me, Sophie."

Flash. My eyes were closed, but the flash of bright white light was still nearly blinding. In my head I heard Marmaduke, his voice garbled, disjointed. He was calling me. Then he sent me images. They came fast, like photo shots displayed briefly in my mind, but it was enough for me to understand. He'd gone to talk to Jina and keep her from ruining my date with Cal. She was responsive at first, but then she grew angrier and angrier, eventually pulling him into a vortex that now held him prisoner.

Tears streamed down my face. Over and over, I could feel and hear Marmaduke begging for my help.

"I'm here, Marmi! I'm here. Don't go anywhere!" I called out, opening my eyes and locking onto his. I must have created some sort of link, because he blinked.

To my left, Astrid was reciting a string of words that made no sense.

I worked to keep my connection to Marmaduke strong. "Marmaduke, hang on!"

Another blinding flash accompanied by the intense, piercing screech and a sharp pain in my stomach as if someone had rammed a spike through me. I grabbed my middle and fell into a heap on the floor.

"Stop!" I heard Cal yell.

"So-oh-ph-ieeeee..." Marmaduke called to me.

"No!" I shouted to keep Cal from halting our progress. "I can—" Another acute pain tore into my shoulder. It felt like someone or something was taking a bite out of me. I grunted through the agony.

Astrid was chanting, the room spun. Cal shouted and shook me. I was vaguely aware of Mrs. Wiley talking to Jina in a calming tone.

The experience was worse than any nightmare that I'd ever had in my life. Coming into a mess like this without a plan that we knew would work was not the smartest idea in the world. The pain in my stomach grew and grew, radiating outward, and just when I thought I couldn't stand it anymore...it stopped.

Everything stopped.

CHAPTER EIGHTEEN

My pain was gone as if it never had existed. The terrible sound in my ears – vanished. Everyone in the room was silent.

Cal tapped me lightly on the shoulder and whispered in my ear. "Sophie. Look."

I uncurled from my fetal ball to look at the ceiling, which was now just a ceiling. Marmaduke stood, perfectly fine, behind the reception desk. I started to call out to him, but Cal stopped me.

"Shh," he said, then pointed to the left of the desk at the beginning of the hallway.

There, on his knees and weeping, was Jonathan, staring up at a visibly lighter, happier Jina. She looked at him with so much love and warmth that I ached for the both of them. "Jina, I miss you. Don't leave me again."

"I know," she said, reaching out to him. She was fading away. He knew it. We all knew it. "I know you miss me, Johnny. But you need to move on."

"We would have had a child. We would have gotten married and had a family. How can I move on?"

"There is no would have, Johnny. There's only what is. And you need to keep creating what is."

She was as thin as the thinnest tissue now.

"Jina!" Jonathan bawled. "I love you."

Having evaporated completely so that all any of us saw was hallway, her final words lingered. "I love you too, Johnny. But there's another who loves you, too. Reopen your heart. Your future is rich."

For the longest time, no one said anything. Cal helped me sit up and squeezed my hands tightly.

Astrid knelt on the floor to console Jonathan, her arms wrapped around him as his body heaved from sobbing.

Mrs. Wiley, her hair whipped into a frenzy around her head, released a heavy sigh and fell back against the wall. "It seems I wasn't needed for communication to occur here. You did just fine on your own. Young lady," she said, somewhat as an afterthought, "promise me you'll never go on the Internet again." She closed her eyes, then reopened them and added, "Ever."

Astrid nodded and continued to rub Jonathan's back while his sobbing slowed.

"I'm not sure about the communication, but I know this wouldn't have ended well without you, Mrs. Wiley." Cal pulled me to stand. "Thank you."

She gave him a faint smile, obviously worn out from the ordeal. "How are you Sophie?"

"I'm good. I swear though, it felt like something bit me." I pulled my t-shirt back from my shoulder and craned my neck to look. "Do you see anything?"

Cal's eyes widened. He skimmed the skin on my shoulder with his index finger. "I can't believe this. It looks like a bite mark."

"Marmi, do you remember anything?"

"Do I remember anything? Does a bird remember a migration route? Does the salmon remember where to spawn? Does a mother remember—"

"Oh boy." Cal rolled his eyes. "Someone's back to normal."

"Sir, my dearest Sophie, sweet, kind Mrs. Wiley, let me just say that I found myself perched on the edge of a precipice that descended into what surely must have been Hell. That is the only reasonable explanation. The screams and moans of lost souls, arms reaching, scratching, attempting to pull Jina and myself into their foul, morbid misery. I do believe now, that Evil incarnates, and it arises from that pit of doom."

Jonathan and Astrid moved to a pair of chairs and sat huddled, comforting each other. "I'm sorry," said Astrid. "It's all my fault. I brought her back, and then I kept making it worse."

Mrs. Wiley patted Astrid's arm warmly. "We don't really know that dear. True, you brought her here, but how this ensued... you can't be sure." She ceased the patting and reached to her hair, working it into something presentable. "But truly, I mean it about the Internet. And witchcraft. Stay away from it all. Obviously not for you." She adjusted her shirt. "If we're done here, there are two boys at home who need dinner."

"Thank you," everyone sing-songed in unison.

"Sophie," sighed Marmaduke. "You saved my very soul today. I am forever in your debt. But for now, I should like to rest." He faded from sight.

"You're not leaving me, are you Marmi?" I yelled out, slightly panicked. Until I almost lost him, I didn't realize what a wonderful friend he was.

He reappeared, but just for a moment. "No, my friend. I shall not. You, as I have heard you say before, are stuck with me." He smiled weakly, and disappeared again.

After putting the office back together a third time, we bid Jonathan and Astrid goodbye and good luck, then headed back to my place, stopping first at my favorite pizza spot for a large New York pizza to go.

As the morning began, with Cal and I eating breakfast at my little kitchen table, so our evening was ending, with the two of us scarfing down some really good and greasy dinner. I was hoping the food would help abate the pounding head-ache that had snuck up on me during the drive home.

It did help a bit, but not entirely. I went to the bathroom, took two aspirin, then decided, just in case, to brush my teeth. I did it as quietly as possible. Didn't want to seem anxious or any-thing. Then I swished some mouthwash around in my mouth just for good measure.

When I returned, Cal was standing by the door. My heart sunk.

"You're going?"

"I probably should. Work tomorrow and everything. But I want to make sure you're okay."

"Eh. A little headache. I just took two aspirin. Guess I'll hit the sack early."

"I uh..." he laughed, not finishing his sentence.

"What?"

"I was about to say that I had a good time today." He laughed some more. "At least it started out good, right?"

"Started out really good," I agreed. "Ended... I guess it ended well, despite the little hiccup."

"Those two – Jonathan and Jina. They were really in love. Young, but really in love."

"Yeah. I hope he moves on like she told him to."

Cal nodded. "Yeah."

I pondered the idea of being bold and asking Cal to stay a while, but didn't quite have the courage to spit it out.

Luckily, Cal bridged the gap between us. He looked into my eyes. "I, uh..." nervously, he glanced down at his hands, then back to my eyes. "I'm finding that I'm very attracted to you."

Stepping closer, until I could feel his breath on my face, I responded profoundly. "Yeah?"

Slowly, our faces gravitated toward each other. He brushed my arm with his hand. "At least you're not running from the room screaming." His mouth pulled into that adorable crooked smile.

I shook my head. My knees were wobbly and my heart pounded so loud I could hear it in my ears. I licked my lips. "No. I'm finding that I'm very attracted to you, too." It was going to happen. We were going to kiss and I was so, so ready. "Very," I added. "It must be your soap."

"Must be," he whispered before touching his soft, warm lips to mine.

Hallelujah! He was a good kisser! Scratch that. He was a great kisser. An exceptional kisser. A phenomenal... Oh no, I was starting to think like Marmaduke. I reached up, pulled his face down and went in for longer, deeper, spine-tingling, and spectacularly arousing lip-lock. His lips were tender but confident, and when he gently brushed his tongue over my bottom lip, I moaned.

He pulled away from the embrace just a bit and smiled. He kissed my nose. "That was nice."

"Yeah," I agreed. "Cured my headache." I didn't mention that another part of me ached now, the sensation far more agreeable.

We both breathed heavily and I know we both desired more than another kiss. I caressed his face with my hand. He took my hand, kissed it, and held it tight. "Sophie," he said, pulling away slightly more. "I've been wanting to tell you something."

I tried to suppress the flinch. The infamous *I've-been-wanting-to-tell-you-something* can never end good. *I've been wanting to tell you something: I'm gay.* Been there done that. Although he didn't kiss like he was gay. *I've been wanting to tell you something: I'm bisexual.* I hadn't heard that one before, but there's always a first time. *I've been wanting to tell you something: I'm an alien from the planet Zork.* Hey, I'd just spent the afternoon rescuing two ghosts from the claws of Hell brought on by an internet spell gone wrong. Anything was possible.

I swallowed. "Is it bad?"

He coughed. "No, no. Not really... it's just kind of hard to say."

"What?"

He closed his eyes, squeezed them tight, then opened them and gazed into my eyes. "It's just... the office." He spit out the last two words and I wasn't entirely convinced by his statement, but I went with it.

"You mean that we work together? I mean, that I work for you? You think it's a problem?"

"No! No. I was, uh, meaning, the office and struggling to get it off the ground. It's been stressful. I just think we should take it slow. And you're right, especially since I'm your boss." He nodded as if this strengthened his argument. "I'd like to take you out again – soon – but we should probably, you know, go slow. Until... until the office is, uh, settled."

"The office settled?" I shook my head. "I don't know what that means."

"Does it matter?" He leaned in and kissed me again, slowly, softly.

I guess not, I thought. Reading between the lines, I figured he was talking about sex. Sure, I could wait. A while. I leaned into the embrace and let myself enjoy. If he wanted to wine and dine and romance me who was I to argue? Better than beer and shots at Barney's anytime.

When we'd finally pulled ourselves from each other's lips and Cal had left for the night, I locked the door behind him and leaned into it, smiling so widely my cheeks hurt. He sure was cute. And way sexier than he seemed when we first met.

"Marmi?" I called out quietly.

He didn't appear, but he talked to me. "Yes, Sophie."

"He kissed me."

"That's good. I am so very happy for you."

"Are you okay?"

"Just peachy. Resting. Standing at the gates of Hell takes some energy from a soul."

"Thank you, Marmaduke."

"For what?"

"You know what."

"You're most welcome."

"Good night," I said.

"Good night, fair Sophie. Sweet dreams."

CHAPTER NINETEEN

I did dream some wonderfully sweet dreams, and while I phys-ically drove to work in a hot and cranky car, mentally I was flying on Cloud 9. I arrived before Cal – I had to remember to call him Dr. Callahan in front of patients – made his coffee, listened to messages, wrote up his schedule for the day and placed it in his exam room with a sticky note attached that said *Have a good day, Doctor.* I drew a heart under the word Doctor. It was so cute and silly. Five minutes later I decided it was too silly, ran into the exam room, and ripped it off before Cal arrived. Best to keep things professional in the workplace, I reasoned.

I was on the phone scheduling a new patient exam when he walked through the door with a briefcase in one hand and some odd piece of equipment in the other.

He smiled, but no more than he did on other days. He gave me a nod and rushed past. When I was done making the appoint-ment, I wondered if I should get up and be the first to break the ice or if I should wait for him to be the brave one. Suddenly, I was feeling awkward and unsure of how to handle myself.

This business of dating and working as employer and employee was going to be worse than I thought. But, I told myself, it was all just a matter of learning how to roll with it. Like getting up on a pair of ice skates for the first time – we'd lose our balance a few times, maybe fall on our butts once or twice, but we'd get the hang of it soon enough. However, since he seemed a little distracted when he came in, I decided to hang back and let him be the first to get out on the ice.

With only a few minutes before our ten o'clock patient was supposed to arrive, Cal appeared at the desk, coffee cup in hand. "Hey, thank you again for making the coffee. It's nice to have it waiting. But really, don't feel like you have to do it every day."

"Don't mind at all. It's all part of my routine now. Lights on, coffee made, listen to messages... wow, I just realized that tomorrow I will have been working here a week. Don't take this the wrong way, but it feels like it's been longer."

"Yeah. Know what you mean."

"So..."

"So..."

"Light day of patients."

"Yep."

"Hope that changes soon."

Boy, he was worried about the office. I wondered if he was worrying about affording me. Maybe I was too expensive to keep on. Ah geez, the complications of mixing romance and work just became more and more apparent. "I'm digging into that project – the letters to optometrists. Should have it done today. Hopefully that will help."

"Yep." He sipped from his coffee and watched me. He cocked his head after the sip. "So, last night."

I nodded. And smiled, although I held it back as much as possible, again, avoiding that whole desperation factor. Desperation is never an attractive feature in a man or a woman. "Last night. It was... nice."

"Yeah, yeah, it was. But, uh, there's still something—" He was interrupted by the door opening. A woman and her daughter – our ten o'clock patient.

Darn! I turned on my bright, welcome-to-our-office smile. "Is this Danielle?" I asked the duo.

"Yes it is," said the mother in a cheery voice. "Hello Dr. Callahan, how are you?"

"Good, thank you. It's nice to see you both again." He slid me a glance. "I'll go prepare for the exam." He turned his attention back to Danielle and her mom, "I'll get you going in just a couple of minutes."

Danielle excused herself to go to the bathroom.

"Mrs. Burgess, has any of your information changed? Address, phone number?" I asked the mother.

"Nothing." She gave me a quick once over. "You're new."

"Yes."

"Do you like it here?"

"Very much."

"We need more eye doctors like him. I want to write some sort of testimonial – something you can give to other patients considering vision therapy. We've just seen so many changes with Danielle. Last week, she just finished reading her first book."

I found that hard to believe. Danielle was... I took a quick peek at her file. She was sixteen. "But she's in high school, right?"

Mrs. Burgess nodded. "Eleventh grade."

"She'd never read a book before?"

"Never. She couldn't do it. Said the words floated around on the page."

"How did she do book reports? How does she study?"

Mrs. Burgess's eyes began to swell with tears. "She talked to friends, asked them about the stories, then she'd wing it. She's been winging it her whole life. And barely passing." She was full-out crying now. I handed her a tissue and had to fight back my own tears.

"Teachers called her lazy for years." She dabbed at her eyes. "I can't let her see me crying. She'll kill me." She reached for my hand and squeezed. "But she's so happy too. Won't admit it, but when she finished that book, she cried too. Then tore right into another one." She rolled her eyes. "Some vampire book. Who cares? She can read about ghosts and witches and goblins for all I care. As long as she's reading."

Cal and Danielle arrived back at the front desk at the same time. "Are you both ready?"

He took them back to his exam room and Marmaduke appeared at my side. "My, my. More accolades for Doctor Wonderful. Or shall we call him Saint Callahan?"

I was relieved to see Marmaduke back to his old self. Feisty and verbose. "I thought you liked him."

"I do. Just having a bit of fun."

The phone rang. "Dr. Callahan's office," I answered with a friendly, professional voice I'd adopted well over the last few days.

A woman on the other end barely let me finish with my genial greeting. "Let me speak with Dr. Callahan."

Geez. She didn't say please. Can't say I liked that. "He's with a patient," I said, remaining as friendly as possible. "Can I take a message?"

"No, you cannot take a message. Put me through to him."

"I'm sorry, but Dr. Callahan doesn't take phone calls when he's with patients unless it's an emergency." Technically, I just made all of that up on the spot, but it seemed like how he'd like things done.

"It's an emergency," she said bluntly.

I really didn't care for this woman or her attitude, but I supposed I had to take her claims of an emergency seriously.

"Are you a patient?"

"This is his wife."

CHAPTER TWENTY

With shaking hands, I punched the hold button and slammed the receiver down. I contemplated my options. I could buzz him directly through the phone intercom system, since I'd learned how to use the convenient function. But then I wouldn't be able to see his reaction. And he wouldn't have a chance to be the recipient of my seething and furious glare. He thought Moonflower was violent? He hadn't seen anything yet. I took several cleansing breaths.

"Sophie? Is there a problem?" Marmaduke asked.

"He's..." deep breath. I shook out my trembling hands. "He's..."

"He's what?"

"He's," I gulped. The word hurt to say. "Married."

"Forget what I said. I do not like the man any longer. I despise the cad."

The phone beeped at me, reminding me that someone was on hold. Ah geez. For half a second, I considered picking up the line and "accidentally" disconnecting it. Instead, I took another breath, picked up the receiver, and buzzed Cal's exam room. "Dr. Callahan?" My voice cracked noticeably.

"Yes, Sophie," he answered through the intercom. "What is it?"

I could have dragged my announcement out so the one-two punch would have been stronger, but I decided to just say it and say it fast. Like ripping off a band-aid. "Your wife is on line one. Says it's an emergency."

The silence on the other end certainly was predictable, if nothing else. "Uh," he mumbled finally. "Thanks. I'll take it in the vision therapy room."

I heard his exam room door open and close, then his footsteps moving toward the vision therapy room further down the hall. The red hold button blinked at me, mocking me. I fought back tears. The sound of his footsteps didn't make it as far as the therapy room though. He'd turned around and was heading back down the hall. He stopped at the desk.

"If it isn't Doctor Debaucher," hissed Marmaduke.

"I can explain, Sophie," said Cal. "I... I can explain."

The phone beeped again. I pointed to it and whispered through gritted teeth. "That's the second warning beep. Next time it rings back, I'll have to answer it and tell *your wife* why you haven't picked up yet." I filled the words *your wife* with as much verbal venom as possible without actually spitting. "What should I tell her?"

He threw his hands in the air, then slammed his hands on the counter and waggled his finger at me. "You'll understand when I explain." He tore back down the hall and I heard the vision therapy room door slam. And the light for line one turned from red to green.

I bolted upright from my chair and paced behind the desk. Should I stay? It was my job. I was earning a paycheck each week now. I had mouths to feed other than my own, rent to pay, and after this, a big bottle of wine to buy. I liked that Sauvignon Blanc. I'd drown myself in it.

"I understand this is a trying time, Sophie, but will wearing a hole in the rug solve anything?"

"It helps me think."

"What, if you don't mind my prying, are you thinking?"

"I'm thinking that I made a big mistake. You were right all along. I never should have fallen for him." I whapped myself on the forehead with my palm several times. "Stupid, stupid, stupid."

"I hardly think that self-abuse is the answer."

I'd been down the married-man road before. And even though I'd gotten over the cheating creep long ago, the pain of the whole affair came flooding back on me like rushing waters through a broken dam. The tears were impossible to hold back. I grabbed my purse, and despite every sane thought that told me I was an adult and should act like one, I acted like a child instead, and ran out the door.

It was too early in the day for wine, beer, or whiskey drinking, no matter how depressed I was, so I stopped at Quickie Mart for a different approach: a two liter bottle of soda, a giant bag of Twizzlers, and a box of Ho Ho's. What I couldn't do with alcohol, I'd achieve with sugar.

The man behind the counter must have felt sorry for me, watching me sniffling and crying as I walked the aisles, because he threw in a giant Snickers bar on the counter and said, "My treat, lady. And just remember, there's always more fish in the sea."

"How did you know?" I sniffled.

"Hey, you think you're the first jilted chick to make a sugar run in the middle of the day?" He looked me up and down. "Only usually they're wearin' sweats and a dirty t-shirt." He mimed his hands around his head. "And their hair don't look so good."

I blew my nose. "Well, I wasn't jilted, exactly, but..." sniffle, sniffle "... same thing, I guess."

I paid, thanked him for his generosity, and departed in the middle of another blubbering outbreak.

As I was about to back out of my spot, I remembered I didn't have cable television anymore. A woman couldn't mourn a romance, even one that had barely lifted from takeoff, without watching some really depressing movies. So I jumped out and got three DVDs from the Dollar-a-Day DVD just outside the Quickie Mart's door. I didn't even pay attention to the titles – I made my decision entirely from description. DVD number one: *Keep the Kleenex nearby for this tear jerker.* DVD number two: *This movie would make Chuck Norris cry.* And DVD number three: *The saddest movie you'll ever watch in your entire life.*

Marmaduke appeared next to me as I sped home. "Sad movies Sophie? Truly? Do you think it wise?"

"I'm not doing crack cocaine. Sad movies are emotional detoxins. I'll sink so low and cry so much that the only way out is up. I'll take them back tomorrow, buy three comedies, and laugh my way out. This is how women work. And where have you been? Don't leave again. I need you right now."

"You need some warm-bodied friends. And what, pray tell, is crack cocaine?"

He was right about the human friends. How pathetic was I? All I had for friends was a dead guy and two animals who probably only loved me for the nuts and kibble I put in their bowls. I started bawling all over again.

I polished off one and a half liters of the two liter bottle of soda, and nearly the entire bag of Twizzlers during the first movie, which really was the saddest movie I'd ever watched in my entire life. In fact, I had to drink three glasses of water to re-hydrate. Then I fell asleep during the second.

The sugar must have really put me into a coma because Marmaduke had to rouse me by yelling in my ear. It wasn't until I was rubbing my eyes that I realized the doorbell was ringing and that someone was pounding on my door.

"The doctor is here," said Marmaduke, "and I think you should give him some heed."

"What does that mean?" I could hear Cal shouting my name through the door.

"It means, let him in."

Most of me wanted to do exactly that. Let him in and wrap my arms around him, smother him with kisses, and never let go. Married? Pshaw. Minor obstacle. The tiniest part of me – the smarter part – knew nothing good came of married men and that I should barricade the door with every piece of furniture in my apartment.

The part of me that ached to kiss every inch of Cal's body stumbled to the door and put an eye to the peep hole. He held a huge brown grocery bag in one arm while he knocked and rang with the other hand.

"Sophie!" he yelled. "Let me in! Please!"

"I don't allow married men in this apartment. Are you married?"

I saw his shoulders sag. "Yes! But if you'll let me in, I can explain. Please let me in!"

Mr. Franklin's door across the hall flew open. My burly and very hairy neighbor appeared, his bushy eyebrows expressing his displeasure. "For crying out loud, Sophie! Let the man in! I can't hear my football game."

My tummy grumbled. "What's in the bag?" I yelled.

"Dinner," said Cal.

"He brought you dinner," hollered Mr. Franklin. "Now would you let the man in and let me get back to my game?"

"Sophie," urged Marmaduke. "I do think it would be wise to hear the man out."

I leaned against the door. "He's married, Marmi. I am not doing that again."

"He's getting divorced."

"How do you know?"

"I had a chat with the man when you fell asleep."

"Well, I've heard the getting-divorced line before. They say they're going to ask for a divorce, but that's just to keep you hanging around."

"The man isn't asking for a divorce, he is in the middle of obtaining one. And I can see why. The woman is a she-devil."

"You're taking his word for it?"

"She came by his office while we were talking. Sophie, he needs rescuing from the horrid beast. She makes Medusa look like St. Bernadette."

I turned and peeked through the hole again. Cal had stopped knocking and ringing, but he hadn't left. He was talking to Mr. Franklin.

"You're getting divorced?" I shouted.

He spun around and put his face close to the door. "Yes."

"He's getting divorced, Sophie!" shouted Mr. Franklin. "His wife is a witch. Trust me, I've been married to a couple of really nasty wenches. They'll steal your soul. Give the man a chance. He needs a nice girl like you."

"You're sure about this, Marmi?"

He nodded. "Open the door."

Slowly, hesitantly, I pulled the chain off, twisted the deadbolt, turned the lock on the doorknob, and did as Marmaduke said. "What's for dinner?" I asked.

Cal rushed in, dumped the bag of groceries on the table, hugged me tight, then pulled away, but held onto my shoulders. "I am so sorry."

"Close the door," I said, sure to keep my tone tight. This was no time to be a wuss. "I don't need any other neighbors knowing my business."

Without taking his eyes off of me, he swung the door closed with one hand, then placed it back on my shoulder. "I am so sorry."

"You said that already." He was melting my heart with his sad blue eyes. He really was sorry. It was written all over his hang-dog face.

"I'll say it again: I am so sorry."

"Why didn't you tell me?"

"I tried. But you're so..." he cupped my face lovingly with his hands. "And she's so..." he made a freaky face and stabbing motion with his hand like he was holding a knife. "Psycho. She's really psycho." He paused. "The trip to the falls – I was going to tell you there, but if you remember, we were kind of interrupted. Then later, when we kissed, I tried to stop myself and tell you then, but you're..." He widened his eyes. "You're such a good kisser. And you're so..."

I crossed my arms. "I'm so what?"

"Amazing," he said on a sigh. "You're the most amazing woman I've ever met."

Hmm. No man had ever called me amazing before. I kind of liked that. "So that whole bit about taking it slow because of the office. You really meant because of your wife. It had nothing to do with romancing me."

"Yes." His eyes widened in terror. "I mean, no!" He waved his hands in the air. "I mean, yes, because of the wife." He grimaced on the word wife. "And no, because I really do want to romance you. You deserve to be romanced."

"Because I'm amazing."

He grinned. "Yeah."

He certainly was saying all the right things. I wondered if Marmaduke had coached him. I wrinkled my nose at Cal. "You didn't answer my question."

"What question?"

"What's for dinner?"

The man could make a mean spaghetti marinara.

"How did you know?" I asked him, as I unattractively slurped up the last of a noodle from my fork.

"Marmaduke."

I nodded. Figured. "Thanks, Marmi," I said.

Marmaduke sat in a chair between me and Cal. I made him do it. He wasn't pleased to be a chaperone. Which was really funny considering that before Cal, I couldn't keep him away on date nights.

He rolled his eyes. "My pleasure."

Cal reached across the table and took my hands. "Can I explain now?"

I had taken my time showering and dressing while Cal cooked the spaghetti and sauce, figuring if he really was sorry, that was fine, but no reason not to make him suffer just a little bit for not having the balls to tell me sooner.

Learning the hard way with Witchy Poo Wife screaming at me over the phone was not even remotely near the ideal scene. "I suppose I'm ready." I sipped from the juice glass filled with – you guessed it – Sauvignon Blanc. Being poor and new to wine drinking, juice glasses were the best vessels I could offer up. "What's her name?" I asked.

"Rachel."

"How long have you been married?"

"Technically?" He looked into the air and counted silently using his fingers. "One year, nine months, and a few days. But that's just on paper. She took off to Costa Rica with some traveling bartender or something. Three days before our first anniversary."

"And she's back now?"

He nodded. "It's just my luck. He dumped her, so she came back and wanted to reconcile. That was... about four months ago."

"Did you?"

"I tried." He shrugged. "Don't ask me why. Guess I thought a divorce meant I was a failure. But my heart wasn't in it. We split up again, and the divorce was going according to plan until she met a lawyer who told her that her lawyer wasn't serving her right – that she deserved half of my practice in the settlement. Without even reviewing my records, this crook – her new lawyer – found some professional who's estimated my practice to be worth two hundred thousand dollars."

"Barristers," huffed Marmaduke. "The world would be better without them."

The dollar amount did seem awfully high based on the low income I'd seen in the last week. "Yikes," I said.

"It's scary. I could lose everything." He ran his fingers through his hair. "But I didn't want to dump all of my woes on you. I just wanted you to understand that she means nothing to me now. This divorce can't happen soon enough."

I stood and carried my plate to the sink. "So you say now."

"I believe the bloke, Sophie."

I pointed a stern finger at Marmaduke. "Stay out of it."

Cal's face dropped. It took every ounce of energy in my body not to run and comfort him and say it was all just fine and let's just do it on the floor right now.

He turned in his chair to face me. "Do you at least believe me that I wanted to tell you about her?"

"I believe that. I do." I leaned against the counter, but couldn't look him in the eyes. I stared at my toes instead. "But you've got a whole lot going on with this woman, and things can change, I've seen it happen, so I have to..." Say it Sophie. Be strong. Say it. "I have to think about it." I shook my head. "You need to let me think about it."

Chapter Twenty-One

I did think about it. I thought about it all night long and didn't sleep a wink. Thank goodness for that sugar-induced nap I'd taken before the spaghetti dinner. Finally, at five a.m. I got out of bed. Sometimes showers help me sort out my thoughts, so I took another one and sure enough, it helped. Somewhere between the wash and rinse cycle, I made a decision.

By nine twenty-five, I was in the office, sorting mail. The coffee was made, messages taken, patient list written up and placed on Dr. Callahan's exam desk. I drank a cold soda from the bottle. Soon I would dig into the project for bringing more patients in.

He walked in at nine thirty-five. Circles under his eyes. They brightened when he saw me. The door closed behind him and he set his briefcase down, beginning to move toward the desk. "You came."

I held up a hand, motioning him to stop. I'd rehearsed a speech. "Wait," I said, standing. "Hear what I have to say." I took a deep breath and tore in. "I'm here as an employee only. That's it. You're Dr. Callahan and I'm Ms. Rhodes. That's what you're to call me: Ms. Rhodes."

His mouth opened to respond, but I shot him down. "No. Let me finish. This isn't easy." His shoulders slumped. "True, I really need the job. That's mostly why I'm here today. I like this job, I like your patients. But it's more than that. I believe in what you're doing. That mother yesterday – Mrs. Burgess – she cried. You didn't just help that girl, you helped her mother. And probably her entire family. It's one thing to have a job. It's another to feel you're making a difference with the job you have. So that's why I'm here."

"So we're through?" he asked.

"We weren't exactly ever started." I waited a beat. "But, if and when your divorce goes through and the court declares that, technically, you are single once again, I'm open to you asking me out on a date." I smiled weakly. "I might say yes."

He shrugged. "That's fair, I guess." He paused, then lifted the briefcase and started toward his exam room.

"And if that wife of yours calls here and talks to me like she did yesterday, I plan to purchase a spell online and hex her bitchy ass."

He smiled. "You have my permission to do that now, if you like." He gave me a small salute. "Ms. Rhodes."

I returned the gesture. "Dr. Callahan."

The next couple of hours went surprisingly well. With the rules laid down clearly, we went about our business. The phones rang, but not enough. He still had gaps in his schedule where patients should have been, but I finished the database of local optometrists and, after having Dr. Callahan approve the letter, did a mail merge and printed them out. Between the three local towns, there were over two hundred optometrists – none of whom did vision therapy in their own practices. The letter encouraged them to refer young patients with symptoms of developmental vision problems.

I stepped out during lunch for stamps, and by two in the afternoon, all of the sealed envelopes were filed neatly in a box ready to go to the mailbox. I sat in my chair proud and pleased, but unfortunately a familiar throb started in just above my eyes. I closed them, and pressed my palms against my forehead.

"Headache?" Cal asked.

I jumped only because I hadn't heard him come down the hall. I did love hearing his voice though. The sound of it gave me a little tingle. I gave a slight nod. "Yeah. It will go away soon." I waved a hand dismissively. "I can work through it."

He motioned to the phone. "Put the message machine on. My next patient isn't until four. I'm giving you an exam."

Hearing his voice was one thing, but sitting in a chair with him looking deeply into my eyes, even if for medical purposes, felt way too close to personal. We were supposed to be avoiding personal. At least, *I* was supposed to be avoiding personal. Business. Strictly business. "I'm fine, really," I started. "I don't think—"

"No arguments." He picked up an empty patient folder from the stack I kept on my desk. "Let's go." When I didn't move, he cocked his head in playful seriousness. "You don't want to be my most difficult patient of the day, do you?"

The lovesick part of me that ached to be close to him, returned his gesture with a restrained grin and pressed the message button on. "Whatever the doctor orders," I said, following him down the hall.

"My job would be easier if all of my patients had that opinion."

In his exam room, I slipped into the big chair, a little intimidated by the instruments perched on metal mechanical arms that sprung like monster limbs from the rectangular unit to my side. It occurred to me that if I was intimidated, his young patients must be terrified. Yet they all bounded from his room happy and unscathed – a testament to his gift working with kids. Sigh. If only I'd fallen for an ol' meanie who sent children screaming, it'd be much easier to sit through this exam.

Cal took a seat on his rolling stool, pen, paper, and patient folder in hand. He scooted closer while scribbling. Finally, he looked up at me. "When was your last eye exam?" To his credit, he was being very professional. That was good. Despite my desire to curl up next to him, settle into the crook of his arm and kiss his neck, his professional attitude was... good.

"Eye exam?" I mimicked. He had me stumped on the first question. Had I ever had an eye exam? I didn't think so. Oh wait – when I was younger... "At the pediatrician, when she had me read the wall chart – was that an eye exam? If it was, I'm not sure I could tell you how long ago that was. Obviously a while. I'm sort of past the pediatrician phase," I laughed.

He rolled his eyes. "That's definitely not an eye exam." He scribbled some more, then looked up again, scooting closer. My heartbeat skipped a couple of times as his proximity neared. I could smell him now and I was getting a little dizzy. "Remember that résumé you said I never read?"

I nodded and tried to hide a swallow.

"I read it last night. You never finished college. Why?"

"You were reading my résumé last night?"

"You answer my question first."

"What was the question?"

"You only completed three semesters of community college."

Touchy subject. I'll admit, I was a little miffed he was bringing it up. "I wasn't doing very well. It didn't seem worth the money. What does that have to do with my eyes?"

"Did you have trouble in high school?"

"Not really. I mean, I was a mostly B student, you know. But I worked really hard for those grades. Harder than most of my friends that made A's. I just don't think I'm exactly cut out for school. Wait, you're not going to want me to get a college degree for this job are you?"

"No, no. This is all about your vision. Those headaches you get – are they mostly on the front of your forehead, over your eyes?" He pointed to his own forehead to illustrate.

"Yeah..."

"Do you ever experience any double vision when you're reading or just after reading?"

"Sometimes. But isn't that normal?"

He shook his head over that little crooked smile. "No. It's not normal." He scribbled some more. "But don't worry, I think we can save you." He winked, and picked up a metal wand with a marble-sized ball at one end. "Follow the ball with your eyes." He waved the thing around while I did as he instructed, not finding it as easy as one would think. He stopped for more note taking, then held it up again. "Now, I'm going to bring this toward your nose. Watch the tip and tell me when you see two balls instead of one." He did that three times and it all went very quickly since the ball split into two for me long before it got to my nose. "Mm-hm," he nodded, placing the wand down and writing more.

"You're doing an awful lot of writing there and not much talking," I complained.

"I'm almost done," he said. Which was really a bit of a fib, because he did all sorts of other tests with small charts and big charts and lenses. Finally, he put the pen and folder down and folded his hands in his lap. "Convergence insufficiency."

I'd seen the word – it was a diagnosis that had to be included on some of the bills I gave patients, but I had no idea what it meant. "What?"

"That's why you get headaches." He brought his two index fingers together forming a V. "Your eyes don't converge easily when you read. So you get headaches. And when your eyes have had enough, they give up altogether – that's when you experience double vision. It's probably why you had to work so hard in high school, and when you got to college, the reading assignments were longer and more intense. I see this a lot." He rolled to his desk, pulled open a drawer and reached in. When he rolled back my way, he handed me a clear bag with a long string inside. On the string were three colored beads. "That's a Brock String – the instructions are on the inside. Read them and do the exercise at home a few minutes each night."

"This little string will cure me?"

"No, but it's a start. You really should do therapy with me a couple of times a week too. Four or five months maybe." Before I could object, he jumped up and snatched a black instrument from his work desk, flipping a switch on it which lit up a small light. "Hang on – I just want to check inside your eyes." The next thing I knew, he had scooted clear up to the exam chair and was in my face with the instrument, looking through his end. We were kissing-close while he moved the thing around, inspecting my right eye intently. I felt his warm breath on my face, and suspected, from the minty scent, that he'd planned this little close encounter. Not that I was objecting. My hand twitched, resisting an urge to reach up and stroke his face, to pull him nearer. "If I didn't know better," I quipped, probably to release my own set of nerves, "I'd say you were making a pass at me."

"Shh, don't move." He switched to my left eye, guiding the instrument around. His skill and intensity only fueled my craving for him, wilting my resolve to keep an emotional distance. Finally, he pulled away. "You're good."

I blinked a few times. "What is that thing?"

He looked at the black thing in his hand, seeming surprised I didn't know. "Ophthalmoscope. It helps me see the tissue in your eye."

"So my tissue is fine."

"Healthy." One corner of his mouth tugged into a sly grin. "I'd consider saying something like, 'It's as beautiful as you are,' but that would be really corny."

It was corny, but my heart jumped into my throat anyway. "Yeah..." Feeling unsure which direction the conversation would lead, I decided getting back to work would be the best thing for calming myself down. I placed my hands on the arms of the chair to push myself up and realized my palms were sweating. Yeah, I really needed to get out of there. "Well, better get back—"

Cal's back was to me, he was slipping his ophthamathingy back into a stand on his work station. "I needed to be near you somehow. Know more about you."

I froze. "Huh?"

"Your résumé. You asked why I was reading it last night. I read over and over again."

My palms were sweating again, my pulse racing. "This exam – another way to be near me? You weren't worried about my headaches?"

He spun around. "No – it was about the headaches. I told you last week when you started that you should have an eye exam."

I relaxed, but only a tiny bit. That was true. He had.

"But I won't lie," he continued. "I liked having the excuse." He hesitated. "To be close to you."

Words – too many words, too many thoughts – choked in my throat. I felt there were two ways to go. Surrender or walk out the door. Walking out the door was harder, but I did it anyway. We stayed out of each other's way the rest of the day.

Chapter Twenty-Two

A t six, just after the last patient of the day walked out the door, Mrs. Wiley walked in. "Hello, Sophie!" she said, out of breath. "How are you doing? Did you recover well from your trauma on Sunday?"

"Mrs. Wiley!" shouted Dr. Callahan from his end of the hallway. "Thank you for coming!"

"Please, please, call me Tara."

My head swiveled from him to her and back. "You asked her here?"

"Yes, she's agreed to sit in on our first meeting tonight."

I gave myself a mental head slap. I'd completely forgotten about the meeting of the misfit group of people and their ghosts. "You're still doing that?" I asked him.

"It does seem odd, since I'm not really in need any more, but they need a place to meet. I didn't have the heart to cancel on them." Of course he couldn't, because he's such a nice guy. If it weren't for that wife, he'd be perfect. "And with Mrs... I mean, with Tara willing to help, it could turn out to be... well, it's something to do anyway." He stopped and frowned slightly. "Wait, you're staying, right?" When I didn't answer immediately, he allowed me an out. "Don't worry. I'd understand if you didn't." The disappointment painted on his face kicked me in the gut.

Tara was feeling the tension. "Did something happen between you two?"

I shook my head. "Long story." Having forgotten the support group date entirely, staying wasn't in my original plans. I had sad movies to return and funny ones to rent. But Cal had that hound-dog, droopy-eyed, crestfallen look going on, and for whatever reason, I felt a sense of responsibility toward the misfit crew about to arrive. I sighed. "Fine," I said. "I'll stay."

I called out. "Marmi, you're joining us, yes?"

He appeared, standing next to Tara. "To watch Edna interrupt poor Stan every time he opens his mouth? Wouldn't miss that for the world."

Everyone agreed that the vision therapy room was the best place to hold the meeting. It was quite large. The only thing we had to move was the round table in the middle. Once that was pushed to the side, we collected more chairs. We brought in all eight from the waiting room, and Dr. Callahan carried in folding chairs he had stored in the back utility room. Along with the five rolling chairs already in the therapy room and my chair from reception, we had enough, hopefully, to accommodate the troubled couples.

Freckle-faced son and ghost father arrived first. They kindly reminded me of their names – Sean and Sean Jr. – and handed me a twelve-pack of bottled water. Right behind them was Pioneer ghost, Cora, and her earthly companion, Dawn. Dawn held a cheese and cracker tray in her hands. My mouth watered. I hadn't eaten since lunch, and that cheese looked especially appetizing. "Where should I put this?" asked Dawn.

I had Sean, Sean Jr., Cora, and Dawn follow me down the hall to the vision therapy room. They oohed and ahhed, all agreeing that the room was more than suitable. I introduced them to Tara. Sean shook her hand warily. "You're not here to study us like that other lady, are you?"

Tara smiled warmly. "No, no. None of that. I'm a medium." She gestured to Sean. "Is this your father?"

He nodded and narrowed his eyes at her. "You see him, right?"

Not offended by his skepticism, she offered a warm smile. "I do. How are you, Sean?"

"Better now, I think," answered the stodgy, cross-armed ghost.

Ghosts and humans were sitting when Dr. Callahan entered. "Hey, Dr. Callahan," said Dawn. "Where's Moonflower?"

"Oh," he looked surprised at the question. "Right. She's, uh, not here anymore."

She raised her eyebrows. "She went into the light?"

He looked to me for help. "Uh, I'm not exactly sure..." The front door opened and the world knew that Stan and Edna had arrived. Mostly because of Edna. "You always make me late," she complained loudly. "Hello!" she called out. "Anyone here?"

"I'm a ghost, Edna, I can—"

"I know you're a ghost you fool, why do you think we're here?"

"Hello!" she called out again. "We brought cookies!"

Dr. Callahan popped his head out into the hall and waved them down.

Edna waddled in, set her plate of cookies on the table next to the cheese and crackers, and let out a deep, heavy sigh. "So sorry we're late." She tipped her head toward Stan. "It's his fault." She looked around the circle of attendees and locked in on Tara. "Who are you?"

Tara stood from her chair and offered a hand to Edna. "Tara Wiley. I'm a medium – Dr. Callahan asked if I wouldn't join you for a meeting to see if I could help at all."

"Help with what?"

"Well, with anything spiritual in nature. That's why you're here, correct?"

Edna waved a hand in front of her perspiring face and sat down. "I'm here because he has problems, not me." She looked up at Stan. "For God's sake, don't be rude, sit down like the rest of us."

"So," smiled Tara, sitting back down in her chair. "You must be Stan. How are you? You feeling okay?"

He shrugged. "Sure."

"Do you mind me asking when you passed from your body?"

He shrugged again, looking a little surprised at the attention. He spoke hesitantly. "It was—"

"Two years ago this October," said Edna. She snapped her fingers. "Went like that. Heart attack. An hour before my Bunco party."

Marmaduke whispered in my ear. "What is a Bunco party?"

"Card game I think," I answered as quietly as I could.

"Dice," corrected Edna. "He ruined the party, and I haven't been able to have one since. He scares all of my friends by moaning and slamming doors and knocking things over. I've tried to tell them that my house is just drafty, but they're spooked anyway."

Stan just shrugged again, but I detected the tiniest curl at the edge of his lip, the evil old ghost.

Tara suggested that we go around the circle, introduce ourselves again, and say what we hoped to get out of a regular weekly "get-together" such as this.

"I'm not sure what that means," said Cora.

"What do you hope to accomplish? For instance," Tara motioned to Cora. "I've often found that spirits remain bound to earth by some unfinished business. If you had some unfinished business, what would that be?"

Cora nodded, her question apparently answered to satisfaction.

Tara started with Sean Jr., who sat directly to her right. Generally, people and ghosts wanted some sort of peace with each other or, like Marmaduke and myself, just wanted to be with others like ourselves. Stan deferred to Edna, explaining that she'd interrupt him anyway, so why bother? Last in the circle was Dr. Callahan, who sat alone, minus the once overwhelming Moonflower.

"I'm – as you can see – without a, uh, spirit now. A ghost. But having been in those shoes, I'm just glad to offer my office as a place to, visit." He clapped his hands on his thighs. "And I guess that's it for me."

"Actually," said Tara, looking over Dr. Callahan's head, "you're not without a spirit. There's one here right now, and she's..." Tara nodded, as if acknowledging something or someone the rest of us couldn't see. "She's been with you for a long time."

His face paled. "What?"

"Do you feel her?"

Marmaduke and I exchanged glances. "What is the woman talking about?" he asked.

Dr. Callahan swallowed hard. "Who?"

"I think her name is Emma?" Then she shook her head. "No, no, she's telling me I'm wrong. It's... Emily. Your sister? Did your sister pass away, Cal?"

He grabbed the seat of his chair.

She continued. "She's what we call a guardian spirit. She straddles the planes, assisting you in difficult times."

Cal started shaking, his eyes grew glassy as they filled with tears.

"She knows this is hard for you, Cal." Tara moved her chair closer to his and covered his hands with hers. "She's talking to me now though, and..." she stopped for a moment, listening to the invisible Emily. "She says that you both need to understand that you're meant for each other." She shook her head. "Do you know what she's talking about. You both?"

My heart lurched. Was Emily referring to Rachel? The beastly wife?

"No," Cal had shut his eyes tight. "I can't do this. Too personal."

A murmur fell over the group and everyone stared above my head. I wrinkled my forehead, wondering what was going on. Tara was staring over my head as well. Her face broke out in a wide smile and she squeezed his hands tighter.

"Oh, Dr. Callahan," said Cora. "Your sister is so beautiful!"

I still didn't understand what was happening. How did they see her, and I didn't?

"I understand your reticence, but she feels this is the right time and place, Cal." With Tara's encouragement, Cal opened his eyes and allowed himself to look. I could tell he was fighting back tears with every fiber of his being.

I'd been craning my neck to get some glimpse of Emily, and finally decided just to stand and turn completely. Cora was right. She was beautiful. Long, wavy blond hair, blue eyes, sweet nose. And look at that. She had a crooked smile too.

"I see," said Tara. "She's explaining now. It's Sophie. She's talking about Sophie."

Cal looked at me, then the vision of Emily, then back to me.

"You answered an ad, right Sophie?"

I nodded.

Tara laughed and looked to Cal. "Did you ever wonder why Sophie was the only one who answered it?"

Now Cal was laughing. A tear rolled down my cheek. We couldn't take our eyes off each other.

"Are you saying that Dr. Callahan's sister was matchmaking?" asked Sean Jr.

My hands shot to my face. I shook my head, crying. "I'm so sorry."

Cal stood and hugged me. "Sorry for what?"

"I don't know. I'm just sorry!" I bawled.

He kissed my cheeks, then my lips, and I nearly forgot we were in the middle of a circle of people watching us.

Tara clapped her hands. "I knew it!" she shouted. "I just knew there was something very special about you two."

"Well I am not happy about this one bit!" yelled Edna. "It's happening again. Just like last time. We get no attention. I'm sitting here with this boob of a ghost man and—"

"Edna!" roared Stan loud enough for angels and demons to hear. "Shut your yammering yap! No one *cares* what you think!"

The group stared in disbelief at Stan, who had finally spoken his mind. During the silence, a light appeared from the ceiling and shone down on him like a spotlight. He looked into the warm luminescence. "Well, look at that," he said. "It's about darn time." He took a moment, basking in the glow. He talked to the light. "Hang on. Be right there." Turning toward his wife, he bent down, and gave a sweet kiss to her cheek. "I do love you, you old gal." He shot me a quick wink, then drifted up into the light. Stan was gone.

And for once, Edna was speechless.

Sean Jr. chuckled. "I guess we know what Stan's unfinished business was."

Chapter Twenty-Three

Whether a guardian spirit had been involved or not, Cal was still a married man. No amount of supernatural assistance driving us together could negate that fact. I kept any anticipation of his divorce in check, but I'll admit, I eased up a bit on my rules of intimacy. On Saturday, sensing my waning resolve, Cal called and invited me on another hike. About halfway along the trail, our hands had managed to find each other, and link. And not wanting the day to end, we dined at a street cafe in Old Town, sipping wine and watching the crowds take in the warm summer night. When he dropped me off at home, I allowed a small kiss. No hanky panky, though. Not until I knew he was truly free.

Did I want hanky panky? Of course I did. I wanted hanky panky *so* badly. It wasn't easy, trust me. After Cal left that night, Marmaduke showed up, and right away, I knew something was wrong. "Sophie," he said. "I think the time has come for us to have a serious discussion."

Thirsty from the wine, I grabbed a glass for water. "About what?"

"Our relationship."

I laughed, thinking he was just playing with me. "Are you breaking up with me, Marmi?"

"Yes. I believe that is the colloquialism."

I turned the water faucet off. "You're serious. You want to leave me?"

"I do not want to leave, yet as time presses forward, I predict my presence will only be cumbersome. Inconvenient. And eventually, wearisome for you and the good doctor. I shan't become the proverbial gooseberry in the room."

Sadly, I considered the context. "Gooseberry – an unwanted person?"

He nodded. My heart sank. Losing Marmaduke wasn't an option.

"You'll never be a gooseberry, Marmi. You're my friend."

"Yes, well I have told you on more than once occasion that you are in desperate need of more warm-blooded companions." He shot a glance at Peter Pan's cage. "The sort without fur."

"That may be true, but it has nothing to do with you." I took a moment to gather my thoughts, since this was the last conversation I expected to encounter. "You told Cal that you thought I was special – that's why you chose to talk to me that first night, at Barney's." I watched his face – it brightened. He nearly cracked a smile. "Am I still special?"

"You most certainly are."

"Then you can't leave."

"You want me to stay, then? You are very positive of this? Should I give you time to think on the subject?"

"My mind's made up, mister. Wanna watch a movie?"

He straightened his jacket lapels, too proud to appear very excited. "I do believe my evening is free." He sat on the couch. "Could we put on my favorite?"

"*Ghost?*"

"You know me so well."

Marmaduke had a good point about the warm-blooded, fur-less companions. I was desperately in need of a girlfriend. Someone to confide in, to share with. In my haste to play the jilted lover, I had closed the door on a dear confidante, so the next day I called Amy and apologized for my behavior. She apologized too and soon we were chatting like the old days. We made plans to get together for a beer and cheesy fries after work the next day – no Shane. Just the girls.

Next, I called someone who I knew really understood me – Tara Wiley. Not only was she a person who could listen, but she could guide me in a direction that I decided was the path for me: exploring my gift as a medium. She would be a knowledgeable and nurturing mentor. A very scary decision, I had to admit. But with the support of two men in my life – Cal and Marmi, who knew where it would take me? The pieces of my life were starting to fall together nicely – finally. And I was pretty sure that, not only was it about time, but that I darn well deserved it.

CHAPTER TWENTY-FOUR

Four weeks later, I was at the reception desk, two lines on the phone holding while I gave a dad new patient forms to fill out for his daughter's initial exam. Cal's days were filling up fast and he had several new vision therapy patients.

The door opened as I was picking up one of the holding lines. In ran Robert and Michael Wiley, followed by their only slightly frazzled mother. Robert was one of our new vision therapy patients. She pointed sternly to one corner. "Boys – sit there quietly. Silently. Meditate for three minutes." She held up three fingers to make her point. "Three." She took a breath then smiled brightly. "Hi Sophie! How are you?"

I waved, and pointed to the phone letting her know I couldn't talk just then.

"How are you, Jonathan?" she asked of the young man sitting next to me.

Jonathan broke away from his computer, a recent new purchase, to throw Tara a wave as well. "Great, Mrs. Wiley. Thanks."

He had stopped by one day to apologize and to offer his services as a website designer. He had time on his hands before heading back for his senior year at college. Cal was thrilled. I know, because we were spending more and more time together. We weren't officially dating. That wasn't allowed yet. I'd set the rules and I was sticking to them. Sort of. But he'd come by to watch a movie with Marmi and me. And he fixed me dinner several nights. If the man hadn't chosen optometry as a profession, he could have seriously considered culinary school. Good looking, great with kids, donated to charities, good cook. The list just grew and grew. So did my lust.

Mr. Franklin, who put on a grumpy face for most, had a soft spot for Cal. They'd even shared a beer once while watching a pre-season football game. Although Cal admitted that Mr. Franklin's place didn't smell all that great, and maybe I could help with making an excuse should he get invited again.

The introduction letters I had sent to the area optometrists worked even better than I had hoped. Several doctors had actually called Cal and arranged meetings. They were looking to send referrals to a developmental optometrist and wanted to make sure his practice was something they could recommend to their patients. Thankfully, they were impressed, and the new patient calls started ringing off the hook. He was filling up with so many patients in therapy that he even started working with two at a time to help offer parents more convenient times after school.

Probably the best part is that one of those parents was a private investigator, who, when he heard Cal's problem with Rachel and the new lawyer, grew suspicious. Having seen some pretty sneaky lawyers in his time, he offered to send one of his investigators out to sniff around.

If he found nothing, Cal owed nothing. If he did, Cal could pay the fee. And guess what?

Turned out Raging Rachel was sleeping with her sleazy barrister. When Cal provided photo proof of their collusion, via certified mail, suddenly they changed their tune. Correction. She changed her tune. And her barrister. With a new lawyer, she was suddenly ready to sign papers with no claims on his business.

Just as I'd finished handling the second call on hold, the vision therapy room door opened and a young boy and girl tore down the hall looking for their respective magazine-reading mothers. They both screeched to a stop beside me first, stood erect, and flashed me gigantic smiles. One of them semi-toothless. That was Becca – she was six years old.

"Do you have lollis for us, Ms. Sophie?" she said with a hint of a lisp.

"Did Dr. Callahan say you worked hard?"

They both nodded vigorously.

"You're sure now?" I teased. I knew they had worked hard. Cal talked a lot about Becca and Patrick – what good patients they were and how much progress they were making. They nodded again.

I pulled two lollipops from my special "Good Patient" cup and handed them over. Patrick snatched his, like a squirrel stealing a nut, and ran. Becca took hers more gingerly and with greater care. Then she reached over and hugged me super tight.

"Thank you, Ms. Sophie." I returned the hug, soaking up the love it contained. The hugs and love of children, I had learned in the last few weeks, was something I didn't think I could ever live without again.

At six o'clock, Jonathan had packed up and was leaving. "See you tomorrow, Sophie," he said. "I probably only have a few more hours work, and then the website should be good to go."

"And then you're good to go, right?"

He nodded. "Yeah."

"When do you leave?"

"Saturday morning."

"I'll bet Astrid will be sad, huh?"

"Yeah. But she's going to visit over fall break. Well, see you tomorrow."

I waved. "Okie dokie."

With all patients out of the office. I got up and locked the door, then grabbed a sealed manila envelope from the desk. It had arrived via courier from Cal's lawyer earlier in the day, but we'd been so busy, he hadn't even seen it. I skipped into his exam room where he was flipping switches and covering equipment.

I waved the envelope in front of him. "Look what came today. Please, please, please be good news." I kissed it for good luck, then handed it over.

As anxious as me, he ripped the envelope and very nearly tore the papers inside. He read silently. I bit my nails while I watched his eyes move across the page.

There were an awful lot of words on that page. He was taking too long. "What does it say?"

He lifted his eyes from the page and looked at me over it, a sly grin on his gorgeous face. "What will you give me?"

"For what?"

"To tell you what it says. What will you give me? A kiss?"

"I'll give you more than a kiss if that says what I hope it says."

"Thirty days."

"And?"

"She's agreed to sign the papers, which she'll do tomorrow. So thirty days from tomorrow, I'm officially divorced."

"And then you're all mine?"

He threw the papers on the floor, hooked an arm around my back, and pulled me in close. "I hate to break it to you, but I've been all yours since I spotted you, lost in the parking lot, looking for Suite A. Now that I believe in ghosts and witchcraft, I think I need to confess to something else."

I looked into his eyes, absorbing the moment. Loving how our bodies fit together so perfectly. As if cast by ethereal molds intending us to eventually join as one. Or maybe I was just being silly. I caressed the line of his jaw with my hand. "What's that?"

"I believe that we are undeniably, indubitably, irrefutably, meant to be."

Or, maybe not so silly. "You're starting to talk like Marmaduke," I teased.

"I'll take that as a compliment." He smiled and took my hand, planting a sweet, soft kiss in my palm that radiated down to the very tips of my toes. My heart melted and so did my willpower. Thirty days. And heck, she agreed to sign... yeah, I was giving in.

We moved the celebration to my place. And lets just say that we took kissing to a whole new *heavenly* plane of existence.

THE END

(or... maybe not...)

A NOTE FROM THE AUTHOR

G hosts may or may not be real, but vision problems that affect a child's ability to learn – they are *very* real. If you have a child, or know of a child who struggles in school, especially with reading, the source of the problem could be visual. To learn more about Developmental Optometry and Vision Therapy, as well as find a list of symptoms, check out the website for College of Optometrists in Vision Development, http://www.covd.org.

About the Author

Karen Cantwell lives and writes in Northern Virginia. As an artist, she dedicates herself to writing fun fiction that entertains readers and keeps them laughing, believing that laughter heals the soul. And yes, she definitely believes in ghosts. She is also the author of the Barbara Marr Murder Mystery Series, featuring danger-prone soccer mom, Barbara Marr. Karen loves to hear from readers, so please visit her website at www. KarenCantwell.com where you will find her email address as well as more information about her and her books.

Other books by Karen Cantwell:

Take the Monkeys and Run, A Barbara Marr Murder Mystery #1

Citizen Insane, A Barbara Marr Murder Mystery #2

Silenced by the Yams, A Barbara Marr Murder Mystery #3

Saturday Night Cleaver, A Barbara Marr Murder Mystery #4

The Chronicles of Marr-nia, Short Stories Starring Barbara Marr

Kiss Me, Tate (Love in Rustic Woods #1)